HIGH JINKS
in
HIGH PLACES

RUTH BARRETT

abbott press

This is a work of fiction. Names, characters, places and incidents are either the product of the author's imagination or are used fictitiously, and any resemblance to actual persons, living or dead, business establishments, events or locales is entirely coincidental.

Abbott Press books may be ordered through booksellers or by contacting:

Abbott Press
1663 Liberty Drive
Bloomington, IN 47403
www.abbottpress.com
Phone: 1 (866) 697-5310

ISBN: 978-1-4582-1935-0 (sc)
ISBN: 978-1-4582-1937-4 (e)

Library of Congress Control Number: 2015913905

Print information available on the last page.

Abbott Press rev. date: 9/29/2015

In memory of my brother
whom I will miss very much

.

CHAPTER 1

J ordan Anderson sat at her desk finishing the final report of a case she had just completed. Looking around, she thought about what she had accomplished in her thirty-two years and where she stood in the career path she had mapped out for herself when she decided to major in criminal law at Harvard University.

She had graduated with a 3.8 grade average and had received offers from a number of law firms, but being a corporate lawyer wasn't what she wanted. Her brother, James, was a JAG lawyer with the navy, and her uncle had been a detective with the Baltimore police department until he was killed in the line of duty. She could easily put herself in their places when they told her how they had conducted interviews and followed leads to arrive at the truth.

It was the thrill of discovering and obtaining evidence and putting the pieces together to make right something that had been wrong that compelled her. She found fulfillment in being a private investigator who chose whether to accept or refuse a case based on the merits and not by political pressure, money, or power. Unlike some of the other private investigators out there, Jordan wouldn't take a case if she felt the person was just looking for revenge or to 'settle a score'. She knew that she had to be able to look back at the face in her mirror each morning. She couldn't do that if she compromised her principles in the process.

She was brought back to reality by the ringing of her phone. "This is Jordan Anderson."

"Hello. My name is Sasha Goldman. A friend gave me your name and number and suggested that I contact you."

Jordan sensed that Sasha was nervous by the soft, almost timid tone of her voice. "How can I help?"

"I work for a large corporation that has a number of federal government contracts. I'm concerned that something's going on that may be illegal. Can you keep this confidential?"

"All my client work is confidential," responded Jordan. "Why don't we meet and you can tell me what's going on."

"That sounds good, but I need to ask you how much you charge. Do you have a flat rate, or do you charge by the hour, or what?" asked Sasha.

"When we meet, I'll give you a sheet that lists my fees, credentials, office address, and phone and fax numbers. I can set up payment plans if that's necessary. Let's see what's involved here. We can discuss the fee later if I take your case."

"I usually visit my parents on Sunday afternoon in Upper Marlboro, Maryland," said Sasha. "Could you meet me for lunch at the Steak and Ale Restaurant on Highway 16?"

"Yes, that sounds good. How about twelve thirty?"

Two days later, Jordan entered the restaurant and noticed a slender, young woman sitting on a bench. She had shoulder-length, brown hair and was wearing a floral-print dress and a pink sweater. The way she was watching people entering the restaurant, Jordan knew this must be Sasha. As she approached and made eye contact, Jordan smiled and said, "You must be Sasha."

"Yes I am." Sasha replied as she stood and extended her hand. "You must be Jordan. I appreciate your meeting me like this."

Jordan briefly grasped her hand. "Let's get a booth so we can talk."

They were seated in a booth near the back of the restaurant. After they placed their orders, the waitress brought them each a glass of iced tea.

"Who recommended me?" Jordan asked.

"My fiancé, Boyd Hutchison. He said you had helped him with a problem he'd had three years ago, and he felt sure you were the person I should talk to about my situation."

"Yes, I remember Boyd. Tell me what's happening where you work."

"The Kingman Corporation develops computer programs that perform multiple functions for naval ships that travel all over the world. They have millions of dollars in government contracts. I'm the executive secretary for Mr. Shaun O'Riley, director of operations."

"Go on."

"When I asked if this would be kept confidential, it's because of my position. I have access to information not available to other staff. I have two daughters, ages three and four and a half, from a previous marriage to support. My husband was killed two years ago while serving a tour of duty in Iraq. He and Boyd were close friends in college and planned to join the navy together, but Boyd wasn't able to pass the physical."

Their conversation was momentarily interrupted when the waitress brought their food. As they ate, Jordan asked, "What do you think is going on at work?"

"Recently, a shipment of cargo being shipped from our warehouse in Arlington to our warehouse in Seattle, mysteriously turned up in Afghanistan. I don't know what the specific cargo was, but it must have been something extremely important because this place has been going crazy ever since it was discovered. There have been private meetings and phone calls every day. Everybody appears very worried.

"A couple of weeks ago, a man came into our office demanding to see Mr. O'Riley. He didn't have an appointment. When I told him that Mr. O'Riley was at a meeting out of the office, he became very angry and agitated. I didn't know what he might do."

"Did he threaten you?" asked Jordan.

"No, but I was sure he didn't believe me. I finally got him to let me set up an appointment for the next morning at nine o'clock. He gave his name as Boris Urich. When I asked the nature of the meeting, he said only that Mr. O'Riley would know what the meeting was about."

Just then, the waitress stopped by their table to refill their iced tea glasses. Jordan looked around and noticed that a number of families were coming in. Looking at her watch, she concluded that the local church services had ended and families were gathering for lunch.

"Had you ever dealt with Mr. Urich before?" asked Jordan.

"No, never. Mr. O'Riley called the office later that afternoon, and I told him what had happened. He was very angry that Mr. Urich had just shown up and behaved like that, but he was glad I'd set up the meeting for the next morning."

"What happened next?"

"The next morning, when Mr. Urich arrived, Mr. O'Riley closed his door, saying that he was not to be disturbed. I heard a lot of shouting, but I couldn't understand what was being said. After the meeting, Mr. O'Riley had me cancel all of his appointments for the rest of the day and said not to disturb him unless it was an emergency."

"What then?"

"He came out of his office twice and was looking through the file cabinet for something. I offered to help, but he just brushed me off, saying that he could find it faster than he could explain what he was looking for. He finally left the office, and I began to straighten up the office and mark his appointment calendar as I always do before I leave for the day. It was then that I noticed them."

"Noticed what?" asked Jordan, noticing the strange look that had come over Sasha.

"I noticed two file folders sitting on his desk. The top one concerned a high-level contract that was up for review and re-funding. The second file was one I'd never seen before."

"Was it also a contract file?"

"No. It appeared to be some sort of a ledger of expenses, but there was nothing explaining how or when the expenses had been incurred. I saw a column of random numbers that may have been some type of code furnishing that information, but that's just a guess on my part.

I was about to mark his appointment calendar when my phone rang. and I went to answer it. While I was on the phone, Mr. O'Riley returned and looked surprised to find me still there. He went into his office and closed the door. When he came out a few minutes later, he asked when I would be leaving. I said that I had only to straighten his office and mark his appointment calendar and I'd be leaving. When I entered his office, I saw only the contract file on his desk."

"Do you think that any of this is connected to the cargo that went to Afghanistan?" asked Jordan.

"I can't be sure, but I believe the cargo involved was connected to the contract that's up for review. From bits and pieces of conversations that I've heard and documents that I've seen, there are serious questions being raised about any and everybody who had anything to do with that contract and whether the contract would be re-funded.

"Mr. O'Riley has been making mysterious phone calls and having private meetings over the past few weeks," Sasha continued. "From what I've overheard in the office, if this situation isn't resolved soon, there could be Senate oversight hearings on the Hill."

Jordan took a drink of tea while she thought about what Sasha had just told her. She was having trouble understanding how the whole matter involved Sasha and what exactly she expected Jordan to do. As she set her glass back down on the table, she fixed her gaze on Sasha. as she said "I can understand why you're questioning some of the things that have taken place, but I'm confused about how any of this affects you and what you expect me to do."

Sasha was very quiet for a moment. "That's a question I have repeatedly been asking myself."

"Take your time" said Jordan, as she placed her hand on top of Sasha's.

"When Carl was killed, my whole world fell apart. It took all that I had to get out of bed each morning, but I had no choice. I had two small children who had no idea that their lives had just taken a huge body blow. Mr. O'Riley and the Kingman Corporation were there for me. I was given time off, with full pay to handle the funeral arrangements and the tons of paperwork. I'll always be grateful for the support that I received. This company and Mr. O'Riley mean a great deal to me."

"I can see that they do," responded Jordan.

"I don't know that there's anything illegal going on. Obviously, something went wrong or some of the cargo wouldn't have ended up in Afghanistan. Everyone who's had even the slightest connection with the contract involving this cargo is under scrutiny. That includes Mr. O'Riley, as the director of operations, and even me as his executive secretary. While I'm sure that Mr. O'Riley would never be knowingly involved in anything underhanded or illegal, bad things have a way of happening to good people. If you'll investigate this, I'll take whatever you find to Mr O'Riley myself, even if it costs me my job."

As Sasha spoke, her eyes did not waver or look away, but remained locked with Jordan's the entire time, showing her conviction and sincerity in what she was saying.

"Let me look into this a little," said Jordan, "and then we can decide who, if anyone, you should contact. Are you all right with that?"

"Yes." said Sasha. "And thank you for understanding."

"What do you mean by mysterious phone calls that Mr. O'Riley made himself?" asked Jordan.

"Normally, Mr. O'Riley doesn't place any phone calls. He'll buzz me on the intercom and have me place the call. I maintain all our clients' addresses and phone numbers for that reason."

"Was he making these calls before this situation with the cargo occurred?"

"No. I noticed that he has what looks like an appointment book that he keeps in his inside suit coat pocket. That may be where he keeps the numbers he calls himself. When he places a call, he tells me that he's not to be disturbed."

"Anything else?"

"About a week ago, he mentioned that he couldn't find a specific file as he was leaving for a lunch appointment. Later that afternoon, I found the file and went into his office to put it in his in-box. He hadn't said that he didn't want to be disturbed, but when I approached his desk, he looked startled and angry about the intrusion and turned whatever he was working on facedown on his desk."

"What did he say?"

"His voice was gruff when he asked what I wanted. I handed him the file, apologized for disturbing him, and quickly left."

"Was that incident typical?" asked Jordan.

"No. He'd never acted that way with me before. When he saw the file, he must have remembered asking about it and immediately came out to my desk and apologized. He said that he had a headache and that was the reason for his attitude. Since it was late in the afternoon, he told me to just take the rest of the day off, so I did."

All the while they had been talking, Jordan had taken notes about the Kingman Corporation and what they do; about Sasha, what her job entailed, and how she felt about her work and her supervisor; and about Shaun O'Riley.

"Let's stop for now," said Jordan. "I want to go over my notes and do a computer search for additional information about Kingman. Before we go, here is the sheet I said I would give you listing my fees, credentials, address and phone numbers. We'll talk more about this at a later time after I have gathered more information. I'll be in touch with you in a few days. Please try to relax, Sasha. Everything will be all right."

CHAPTER 2

Shaun O'Riley was reading some papers in preparation for his meeting with Tom Clancy, vice president over security and disbursement at Kingman Corporation, who was wrapping up a phone call in his office.

Shaun was about sixty, with thinning hair and a build that let you know he was a big fan of two-hour lunches. He took his job as director of operations very seriously. He was a stickler when it came to following procedures and could be someone to reckon with when things went wrong. He was also the person most likely to be named boss of the year. Unfortunately, things had gone very wrong, and he was frustrated. No matter which way he turned, no answer was forthcoming. Now, a Senate oversight committee had gotten involved.

When the light on her intercom went out, the secretary motioned to Shaun that he could enter Tom's office.

The two men shook hands before Shaun sat on a chair opposite Tom's desk. Tom was three or four years younger than Shaun, and he took better care of himself. He was more a soup-and-salad-type of guy who tried to stay away from burgers and fries. He frequently spent weekends in his health club's swimming pool with his grandson.

Today, both men shared the same problem; neither had been able to find a solution. That's why they were expecting George Kilburn to join them.

"That was George Kilburn on the phone," Tom said. "He's running a little behind schedule but will be joining us in a few minutes."

"I'm glad to have a few minutes to speak with you alone," said Shaun. "We may have a problem."

"What happened?" asked Tom. "I thought you said that everything was running smoothly."

"Boris Urich showed up at my office the other day demanding to speak with me. Fortunately, I was in a meeting at the Pentagon. Sasha told him that, but I don't think he believed her. He finally agreed to a meeting the next morning."

"What was his problem?" asked Tom.

"As the disbursement officer, Boris was in charge of sending that shipment to Seattle. Apparently, he's scheduled to meet with George Kilburn sometime over the next couple of weeks, and he has a major case of nerves over it. I told him everything was all right and he needed to relax, but I don't think he will," said Shaun.

"Boris knows that George works for Senator Granger and is an investigator for the Senate oversight committee," Tom said. "If he's that nervous about a meeting with George, maybe we should find out why. Find out what George is concerned about. Let him know you're aware that he'll be meeting with Boris and just want to make sure that Boris has all the information with him that he might need."

Just then, the door opened and George Kilburn walked in. "Sorry to be late. Our staff meeting went longer than I'd planned."

"That's all right," said Shaun. "I was just telling Tom that you're planning to meet with Boris sometime during the next couple of weeks. If you have any particular concerns and don't mind sharing them, I'll make sure Boris has whatever paperwork he might need with him."

"There are no specific concerns with him at this point," said George. "I'm sure you're both aware of the situation concerning the cargo that was supposed to go to Seattle but ended up in Afghanistan."

"Of course," said Tom. "It was an advanced early warning security system along with the actual hardware to be installed onboard U.S. ships being made ready for battle. Once installed, the device would sound an alert if an intruder tried to override or lock onto any of the operating systems onboard the ship."

"Exactly," said George. "I'm just looking through the requisitions and shipping documents to see if there's anything that will give us a clue as to why and/or how that portion of the shipment went astray. Since Boris was the disbursement officer, it seems only right to see if he can shed any light on what might have happened."

"Yes. We're all trying to answer that question," said Tom. "The warehouse manager was the only person in Seattle who was aware that a new security system was even in the works and would be sent to him for a trial run on the ships at the naval base in Bremerton when it became ready. He didn't know, however, that it had been completed or that it was being sent with this shipment."

"As you're aware," said George, "if this was to fall into the wrong hands, the results could quickly become catastrophic. The monetary cost alone would run into the billions, and the potential loss of life could be devastating. Let's all hope this is resolved before it gets that far."

"I'll make sure that Boris brings all the requisitions and shipping documents with him to your meeting," said Shaun. "I feel sure there's a reasonable explanation as to how this happened. Just like you, we want to make sure that it doesn't happen again."

"Great," said George. "I don't expect my meeting with Boris to last more than half an hour. I'll call to let you know the date and time of my meeting with him. I do have one question. While going through documents from previous cargo shipments, I noticed that Chester Rafferty was listed as the disbursement officer. He also signed off on the initial documents connected with this current cargo shipment to Seattle. Shortly before the actual shipping date, Chester's name was replaced with Boris's. I was wondering why."

"I'm sorry," said Tom. "I thought you knew. Chester suffered a massive heart attack and died. It happened very suddenly. No one knew that he was even sick. We were fortunate that Boris had recently transferred here from our warehouse in Philadelphia. He had just qualified for a management position there, but there was some kind of family emergency that made him request a transfer here. He was placed in a job that paid what he had been making in Philadelphia with the understanding that he'd be given the first position that he qualified for in a management position. We were lucky that he was here. He met the qualifications for the job, was already an employee of the company, and had the necessary security clearance on file."

"That takes care of my questions," said George. "Unless you gentlemen have any questions for me, I'll leave you to your work."

They stood and shook hands and George Kilburn was on his way.

"Shaun, can you stay around a few minutes more?" Tom asked.

"Sure, no problem," said Shaun as he sat back down. "What's on your mind?"

"I'm not really sure. It's just that when I was telling George how Chester died and how Boris just happened to be ready to take his place, I got a funny feeling in my gut."

"Well," said Shaun, "I admit that it was quite a coincidence, but I can't see anything that should have raised a red flag. Do you think there was something we missed? Chester certainly didn't plan on dying when or how he did. As far as I know, Boris never crossed paths with Chester. Do you have any information to the contrary?"

"No. As far as I know, the two never met, but I've never believed in coincidences," said Tom. "I'm just stumped as to how that shipment got misdirected. I've been told that George has been directed to make this his top priority. That suggests to me that somebody knows or suspects something that we don't know about."

"That's interesting," said Shaun. "Maybe we should do a little checking into Boris's and Chester's histories to find out if their paths ever crossed. I'll have personnel send me their files."

"Good idea," said Tom. "Have Sasha prepare a side-by-side report beginning with when each man graduated from college and what his major was. Include any military service, where they lived, and every job held since graduation up until Rafferty died. I just have this nagging feeling that we've missed something. Let's set up another meeting after she's completed the report."

CHAPTER 3

Several weeks had passed since Sasha had spoken with Jordan. Whenever she attended a meeting, she would remember what was said and by whom and record the information in a notebook she kept locked in her desk to share with Jordan later. Whenever she was given a document that she thought looked relevant, she would make a copy and place it in a folder that she kept with her notebook.

A week or so ago, she had been given Chester Rafferty's and Boris Urich's personnel files and had completed the side-by-side report her boss had instructed her to prepare. She was making a copy of the report on the copy machine for her file, when her phone rang. She answered the call, leaving the machine running. As she was hanging up, she saw a coworker heading toward the copy machine, which, by this time, had completed her job and stopped. Trying not to panic, she called out, "Hi, Cynthia. I see that my work has finished copying. Let me get it out of your way." She quickly walked to the copier and retrieved the original and her copy. When she returned to her desk and put the copy in her special folder, her heart was beating like a drum at a halftime show.

It was common knowledge that Chester Rafferty had died from a massive heart attack not very long ago and a relatively new employee from Kingman's Philadelphia plant, Boris Urich, had replaced him. Chester had been well known and liked by everyone he worked with. The word had gotten out within the company that a portion of a cargo shipment had ended up in Afghanistan, although the rumors failed to indicate what the exact nature of the cargo was or its intended destination.

Sasha was beginning to get nervous and wondered if she had done the right thing by going to Jordan. She had several important documents and her notes locked in her desk. If anyone found them before she could get them to Jordan, it could mean her job.

On Wednesday afternoon, Sasha had just returned from lunch to find her phone ringing. "Kingman Corporation, Mr. O'Riley's office, Sasha Goldman speaking. How may I help you?"

"Sasha, this is Jordan. I'd like to set up a meeting with you. Are you free on Friday?"

"Yes, I have an appointment to get my hair done at one thirty, but I should be finished by three. How about meeting for a late lunch? There's a pizza and pasta restaurant just down from the beauty shop where we can meet. It's in that new shopping center with the mega Walmart in it."

"I know exactly where that is," said Jordan. "In fact, I've been wanting to try that restaurant. It always smells so good when I pass by."

"It's wonderful. Boyd and I have eaten there several times, and we love it. Mr. O'Riley just buzzed me on the intercom, so I have to go. I'll see you Friday. Good bye."

Two days later, when Jordan arrived at the restaurant, Sasha was already there and in a booth where they could talk without being overheard. The waitress took their order and brought Jordan an iced tea. Sasha already had a beverage.

"I'm sorry that I haven't been in touch before now," said Jordan, "but I've been doing research to find out all I can about the Kingman Corporation and the kinds of government contracts they have. Has anything been happening on your end?"

"Yes," said Sasha as she took out her note pad. "Mr. O'Riley recently attended a meeting in Tom Clancy's office. He's the vice president over security and disbursement. Another man I don't know was also present. His name is George Kilburn. Fortunately, Mr. O'Riley takes detailed notes of all his meetings and has me type them up and put them in a special file. I made you a copy of those notes," she said as she removed the papers from her folder and handed them to Jordan.

While they were eating, Sasha told Jordan about the assignment she had received following that meeting, stopping long enough to remove a copy of the report from her folder and hand it to Jordan.

"Did he give you any indication about why he wanted this report?"

"No," said Sasha. "He just wanted me to do it right away."

"Maybe I'll find a connection after I've gone through the minutes of their meeting," said Jordan thoughtfully. "He must believe there's a connection between these two men that goes beyond just holding the same job. I wonder what that could be.

But Jordan, do you know George Kilburn? You got a strange look when I mentioned his name as if you'd remembered him from somewhere."

"I'm not sure," said Jordan. "Maybe. Do you know any more about him?"

"Only that he works in Senator Granger's office and has something to do with the Senate oversight committee," said Sasha.

"That's him," said Jordan. "I was introduced to him once at a party given by a friend of mine. I didn't get to speak with him for more than a few minutes, but I remember that he made a strong, positive, first impression on me, like he was a man who was trustworthy and had integrity and someone I'd like to know better."

"Jordan, please tell me you aren't going to tell him about this. I can't afford to lose my job."

"Relax," said Jordan. "I'd never do that to you, but this gives me an idea of a way to have a discussion with him on neutral ground. Getting reacquainted with George Kilburn may turn out to be a very good thing. I think it's time for my friend, Beverly, to have a small dinner party and invite George and me. She's always trying to fix me up with someone, so she'll be delighted if she thinks I'm at all interested. I think I'll give her a call tonight and get the ball rolling."

While Jordan was busy laying out the groundwork for her plan in her head, they finished their lunch and left. Sasha headed home, but Jordan had some shopping to do and a suit to pick up from the dry cleaners before she called it a day.

When Jordan pulled into her driveway with groceries and laundry in hand, she looked up to see her tabby cat, Annie, sitting in the window awaiting her return.

Annie was a stray cat that had found Jordan on the day she was moving into her current home. Annie just walked in, looked around, and took charge. At that time, Jordan was also in the midst of establishing herself as a private investigator and wasn't sure she was ready for a cat, but Annie quickly changed her mind.

She was a beautiful, tortoise-shell tabby with very soft, short fur that was mainly a calico mixture of black, light and dark brown with some orange, white, and gray thrown in for good measure. Jordan was convinced that one look from Annie with those big, grey eyes, could melt even the coldest heart and convince you that she was looking straight into your soul. Jordan never stood a chance. It was love at first meow.

By the time Jordan had the front door open and her parcels inside, Annie was there meowing and rubbing against her legs; her way of saying it was past time for her afternoon treat. Acknowledging that Annie's needs were her first priority, Jordan kicked off her shoes, picked up the bag of treats, and headed for their favorite lounge chair. Annie happily purred on her lap as she munched on some treats as Jordan looked over the papers Sasha had given her.

She mulled over her plan to get reacquainted with George Kilburn. She thought back to the party when Beverly had introduced them and tried to remember what he looked like. She had not had much in the way of a personal discussion with him, but she had listened to his thoughts and comments with others in the group. She had been surprised at how much they had in common. She realized that she was really looking forward to this dinner party and the hostess didn't even know she was having one yet.

As Jordan was engrossed in her thoughts, the phone rang. "Hello?"

"Hello, Jordan. This is Beverly. How are you?"

Beverly Wilson had been Jordan's college roommate and sorority sister. Beverly had met Carl Sanders at college and had married him within a month of graduation. Jordan had been Beverly's maid of honor. Carl was about six feet tall and had a strong, muscular frame. He had been a running back for the college football team and still maintained the same weight and build he had had in college. Beverly was a slender, five-foot blonde with curves in all the right places. Being a full-time mother of two active boys—Jason, age seven, and Ben, age four, helped her maintain her college figure.

"Wow," said Jordan. "I'm doing great. Talk about déjà vu. I was just about to call you. How are Carl and the boys?"

"We're all doing well. We just returned from two weeks with Carl's parents in Miami. The weather was great, and the boys loved seeing the ocean and playing on the beach. They want to move there now. Carl and his Dad went fishing and came back with enough trout to cook for dinner one night. We grilled them in the backyard and made a picnic out of it. It was a lot of fun. In fact, that's indirectly the reason I called".

"What do you mean?"

"While we were at the beach, it reminded me of the trip you and I took there while we were in college. The shop that sold those beautiful shells that neither of us could afford is still there. I couldn't resist buying a beautiful conch shell centerpiece for the table. Actually, I got one for you, too, so we need to get together. Now, what have you been up to?"

"Not nearly as much fun as you've been having," Jordan replied. "Work's been keeping me busy as usual. I remember the fun we had on that trip during college and I remember that shop, too.. I can't wait to see that centerpiece. Thank you for thinking of me. Like I said, I was about to call you because I want to ask you about something."

"Okay," said Beverly. "What's on your mind?"

"Do you remember the party you had at your home a few months ago?"

"Sure," said Beverly. "What about it?"

"There was a guy there I'd never met before. He was about six feet tall with brown hair, as I recall. I think his name was John or George something."

"You're talking about George Kilburn. He works in Senator Granger's office. Carl knows him from a bowling league they're in. Are you saying that you're interested in him? He's single, and I think you'd make a great couple."

"Hey, slow down. Don't send out wedding invitations yet. I'm just asking," said Jordan. "As I recall, he was relatively nice looking and had a good personality."

"What made you think about him?" asked Beverly.

"I don't know. Somebody was talking about a party she'd recently attended and that party at your house just popped into my head."

"Carl was just saying last night that he wanted to see that new movie showing at the Grand. How about Carl inviting George and making it a double date? Would next weekend work for you?"

"Yes, I don't have any plans for Saturday. That actually sounds like fun."

"Great. Carl's bowling tomorrow evening. I'll have him mention it to George. I'll call you when the plans are set. Right now, I hear a little boy running around when he should be in bed. I better hang up and go be Mommie. I'll call you soon. Good bye, Jordan."

As she hung up, Jordan was smiling at the way the pieces of her plan were falling into place. The only thing she had to do was to find some way to get George talking about the situation at Kingman Corporation on their double date. *How hard could that be?* she asked herself. The word *impossible* flashed on and off in her mind like a neon sign.

CHAPTER 4

Carl Sanders was getting ready to leave the house. "Beverly," he called, "where's my bowling shirt?"

"Hanging in the closet next to your blue jacket. Please don't forget to talk to George about going to the movie with Jordan this weekend."

"Does Jordan know that you're playing matchmaker again?" he asked with a smile.

"She not only knows," said Beverly, "I think she's even interested. Have a good game."

Carl and George were members of the Potomac Pirates, a group of men who had met at a health club. As they got to know each other, they found that they all had an interest in bowling as well as working out. Thus, the league was formed. Tournaments were held at the local bowling alley. The league winners received a plastic trophy along with a gift certificate for dinner for two at one of the nicer restaurants in the area. After the game was finished, the group usually moved into the refreshment area for burgers and fries or pizza and a beer or coffee. They would shoot the bull for half an hour or so before heading home.

"You bowled a good game tonight, George," said Carl as he sat next to George. "Picking up that split was just short of genius."

"I'd call it exceptional luck," said George.

"You seem to get your exceptional luck every time we come here, especially when I'm on the opposing team."

"What can I say?" said George. "Maybe you just need more practice."

"Tell me something," said Carl. "Are you going out with anyone special right now?"

"Not at the moment. Why do you ask?"

"Beverly and I were planning to see that new movie at the Grand this Saturday and were wondering if you'd like to join us."

"Just the *three* of us? Who's Beverly wanting to pair me up with now?" George asked with a knowing smile.

"She was planning on asking her friend, Jordan Anderson, to join us. I think you met her at a party at our house a few months ago. She's about five four with brown, shoulder-length hair and a slender build."

"I remember her," George said. "She didn't say a lot, but when she did talk, it was worth listening to. I seem to recall that she was quite pretty. Sure, I wouldn't mind seeing her again. Just let me know what time and I'll be there. I don't remember if she mentioned what she does for a living. Do you know?"

"She's a private investigator," said Carl. She works on her own, and from what Beverly's told me, she's gaining a good reputation. Most of her business is from word of mouth, and she seems to keep pretty busy."

"You're kidding. This should be interesting. I've never dated a PI before."

Carl got home, put his bowling ball in the closet, grabbed a cup of coffee from the kitchen, and strolled into the family room, where Beverly was reading a book.

"How was your game?" she asked.

"Good, but my team lost," he said.

"What did George say about the movie?"

"He's available and willing, but he's got your number. As soon as I mentioned the movie, he wanted to know who you were trying to fix him up with this time," Carl replied with a laugh. "George said he remembers meeting Jordan, and I think he's actually looking forward to seeing her again. You just may have made a match this time."

"I hope so. I'd like to see Jordan find someone she can enjoy being with. I'll call her on Monday and let her know."

CHAPTER 5

On Monday, Jordan was in her office going over the notes and documents Sasha had given her when they met for lunch on Friday. She wasn't sure what to make of the side-by-side report that Sasha had been instructed to prepare, but her gut feeling was that it was significant.

Since Sasha had told her that George Kilburn was somehow involved in this, she hoped the movie date that Beverly was setting up would give her the opportunity to gain some further information.

A brief article in this morning's newspaper caught Jordan's eye.

Cargo Takes a Wrong Turn

A shipment of cargo being sent from the Kingman Corporation's warehouse in Arlington to their warehouse in Seattle made a wrong turn along the way and ended up in Afghanistan. It's a good thing the company doesn't manage the postal service.

The article had made light of the situation and didn't indicate what kind of cargo was involved or that the contents were military.

This article should give me an excuse to raise the issue in general conversation without sounding overly curious, thought Jordan.

Her ringing phone brought her thoughts back to the present.

"Hello," she said as she picked up the receiver.

"Hello, Jordan., this is Beverly. I know you're probably busy, so I won't keep you, but I wanted to let you know that Carl spoke to George at bowling last Saturday, and he's agreed to come with us to the movie this Saturday. Carl said that George remembers you and said he's looking forward to seeing you again."

"Good news! Thanks. This should be fun."

"By the way," inserted Beverly, "Carl said that George was intrigued when he found out that you're a PI. We'll pick you up. I'll check with you later in the week to set the time. Gotta run. Bye for now."

Jordan remembered her promise to let Sasha know how things were going. She dialed her number.

On the second ring, she heard "Kingman Corporation, Mr. O'Riley's office, Sasha Goldman speaking. How may I help you?"

"Sasha, this is Jordan. Do you have a few minutes?"

"Yes. Mr. O'Riley's having lunch with a friend out of the building and isn't due back for another forty-five minutes. What's going on?"

"My friend Beverly has arranged a double date for George and me with them next Saturday."

"How will you get him to talk about the Kingman Corporation?"

"Did you see the article about Kingman in this morning's newspaper? Having that article appear this morning is a stroke of luck. It'll give me a reason to bring up the subject without your name being mentioned."

"I like the sound of that," said Sasha. "I've been a little worried since you mentioned you thought you knew George Kilburn."

"I thought that might be the case," said Jordan. "That's why I wanted you to know what I plan to do. It's important to me that I have your trust and that you know I won't do anything that will cause you any problems."

"I do trust you. I can see why Boyd told me that I didn't need to be afraid of talking with you."

"Great," said Jordan. "Be sure to call me if there are any more meetings like the one we discussed or if you come across anything you think is noteworthy. If I'm out of my office, just leave a message. I always check my messages every day even when I'm traveling. No one but I can retrieve my messages, so don't worry about anything you might say. Any questions?"

"No. Thanks, Jordan."

Hanging up the phone, Jordan gathered her things and closed the office. She had some shopping to do before Saturday's date.

By Saturday, she was ready. She was wearing a new dress and shoes and had treated herself to a manicure. She had also had her hair done by her favorite stylist.

At six forty-five, Jordan glanced out the window and saw Carl and Beverly's car stop in front of her home. She picked up her purse and a light wrap and was heading out the door as Carl reached her front porch. Not more than ten minutes passed before they arrived at the theater.

They had just reached the entrance when George walked up. He and Jordan reintroduced themselves, and they headed into the theater. The women waited while the guys purchased two large buckets of popcorn for each couple and sodas all around.

As she was waiting, Jordan used the opportunity to take a good look at George. He looked very nice in his suit and tie, as she knew he would. She was impressed when she noticed that his shoes had a glossy shine. She felt that most men didn't bother about how their shoes looked any more as long as they weren't caked with mud. She had forgotten how handsome he was, and her mind began to wonder how it would feel to have his arms around her. Beverly startled her back to reality when she touched her arm as the guys returned.

When they had settled into their seats, George smiled at her. "You look very nice tonight. I was glad when Carl invited me to come tonight because it gives me another chance to ask for your phone number. I hope you'll give it to me tonight."

"Thank you for the compliment," said Jordan. "I'll be happy to give it to you if you don't mind waiting until I'm not trying to balance popcorn and a drink in my lap." She laughed.

"Agreed," he said.

When the movie was over, Beverly said, "It's too early to call it a night. How about going to that coffeehouse across the street? Carl and I have been there on several occasions and really enjoyed ourselves."

Her suggestion was met with unanimous approval. They checked for traffic and headed across the street.

The coffeehouse was dimly lit. Tables filled the center of the room; and more private booths lined the walls. A band was playing loud enough to be heard but not so loud that people could not engage in conversation. There were candles on each table along with a never-ending supply of shelled peanuts.

The group chose a booth. While they waited for their order of a large mushroom and pepperoni pizza and a pitcher of beer,

Beverly kept everyone laughing with stories of the most recent antics their boys had performed that week.

"I was just thinking," began Carl while looking from Jordan to George, "that you two have something in common you may not be aware of. You are both godparents to our boys. Jordan, you were present when Jason was baptized but weren't able to be there when Ben was baptized. Just the reverse was true for you, George."

Jordan made a mental note that this common bond might prove to be a unique building block in establishing a further relationship with George.

After they finished eating, they ordered lattes to top off the evening.

George looked at Jordan and said "Carl tells me that you're a private investigator. Do you have any particular type of case that you specialize in, or do you take whatever comes along?"

"I'll take almost any type of case if, after talking with the client, I feel that an injustice has truly been committed and the person isn't just trying to get even."

"Have you ever turned down a client because you found out that was the case?" asked George.

"Yes, I did have to do that once," said Jordan. "A man came to me alleging sexual discrimination because his boss had promoted a woman over him who was younger, had fewer years on the job, and was very pretty. He'd been with the company for fifteen years, and the woman had been with them for only four. I found out he had only two years of college while the woman had a master's in business. The man had a reputation among his coworkers for being lazy with poor work habits. He did just what he had to do and nothing more, whereas the young woman went the extra mile to make sure she didn't miss anything. She was always willing to lend a helping hand to anyone else."

"How'd you handle it?" asked George.

"I told the man that in my opinion he'd gotten just what he deserved and if he wanted to pursue it, he needed to hire someone else. That's the type of case I don't need and won't take on."

"Doesn't taking that approach mean you have a sparse workload at times?"

"Yes," said Jordan, "but it also means I can face myself in the mirror each morning. Fortunately, I don't come across that type of case very often. An interesting fact in this case that I found out a week later was that this man had also gone to an attorney and had been turned down there, as well."

"You sometimes get involved in resolving disputes as well, don't you, George?" said Carl.

"Yes I do. Only mine are on a little larger scale."

"Speaking of large-scale issues," said Jordan, "did any of you read that article in Monday's paper about the shipment of cargo that was supposed to go to Seattle but ended up in Afghanistan? I think the article said it involved the Kingman Corporation."

"I didn't see the article," said Beverly, "but they've been talking about it on the news. They didn't say what the cargo was. The reporter was laughing about the comment made by the newspaper that it was a good thing Kingman didn't run the postal service. If it was just a joke, why were they reporting it on the news?"

"Good question," said George. "The whole thing seemed strange to me."

"Assuming that it's true, it sounds interesting to me," said Jordan. "Now that's a case I'd love to work on. There are so many possibilities of things that could have gone wrong or people doing wrong. I'm sure that if it really happened, it would be a difficult case for whoever works on it, but solving a case like that would give any investigator a real feeling of accomplishment."

Just then, Beverly looked at her watch. "Carl, it's time for us to go. The boys will already be in bed, and you need to drive the babysitter home. I still have to get their clothes ready for church in the morning."

They all walked to the parking lot. After exchanging pleasantries, Jordan left with George.

When George pulled up in front of Jordan's house, he turned off the ignition and turned to Jordan. "I had a great time with you tonight, Jordan. I'll definitely have to thank Carl for asking me to come along."

"I had a wonderful time with you too," said Jordan. "Before I forget, let me give you one of my business cards. My number's on the back."

"Thanks. Tell me something, Jordan. Were you serious when you were talking earlier about the types of cases you would or wouldn't take on?"

"Absolutely," she said, looking at him in a questioning manner. "Did you think I was kidding?"

"No, I didn't think that at all," he said. "Please don't misunderstand me. I was very impressed to hear that you operate in that manner. As you might guess, working on the Hill brings me in contact with many different kinds of people. Most of them seem to do what they do because of the money or the feeling of power they get from being around people who are well known. It's refreshing to meet someone like you who has a passion for what she does not for fame or fortune but because she truly believes she's helping others. You have a very rare gift."

"Thank you," said Jordan. "I appreciate that."

George glanced at his watch. "It's getting late. I'll walk you to your door, and then I need to go. I'd like to see you again."

"I'd like that as well," said Jordan. "I hope you'll call me."

"You can count on that." replied George.

After seeing Jordan to her door, George left. All the way home, he thought about the evening's events. He had enjoyed reconnecting with Jordan and getting to know her a little better. She was not only a beautiful person inside and out, but she was very smart and funny. He hadn't wanted to push things, but he couldn't help but wonder how she would feel with his arms wrapped around her. Just thinking about it made him feel very good.

An idea was beginning to form in his mind, but he needed to make some phone calls first. He was sure that if he could put his plan into motion, the coming week would prove to be interesting. *Very interesting indeed*, he thought.

Chapter 6

When George arrived at work on Monday, he checked his calendar to see what meetings he had scheduled for that week. His attention focused on his meeting with the Senate oversight committee scheduled for Tuesday at ten o'clock.

The purpose of the meeting was to brief the committee as to what, if anything, he had discovered about why and how the cargo ending up in Afghanistan, rather than Seattle and his plan of action to obtain this information.

He would also let the entire committee know exactly what the cargo consisted of. A few key members of the committee were already knowledgeable but because the security system was being sent to Seattle for installation and testing, details of the cargo and plans for testing it had been restricted to those who were actually involved in some phase of the operation.

George pressed the intercom button and said to his secretary, "I have some important telephone calls to make, so please don't disturb me unless it's an emergency. Also, please find out if Trevor Johnson is working on anything crucial at the moment and if he can meet me for lunch today."

Trevor Johnson, is an attorney and Senator Granger's personal assistant. He often works with George when he is conducting high-profile investigations that could involve national security.

George finished making his calls and was looking over the information he had accumulated.

Senator Granger's office had initially been contacted by Shaun, stating that he had received a telephone call from the Kingman warehouse manager in Afghanistan, Stanley Fremont. Stanley had advised him that when they received and opened some requisitioned, routine supplies, they discovered some additional cargo in the shipment that had not been requisitioned. When Stanley realized what this cargo was, he immediately had it placed in a secure location and called Shaun for instructions.

Shaun had the requisition and shipping documents for that shipment pulled for his inspection, but he found that they listed only the routine supplies Stanley said they had requisitioned. Nothing in the documents mentioned the security system package.

It was at this point that George had been brought into the picture. His job was to find out how and why this had happened and whether this was an incredible mistake or a masterful sabotage. Until these questions were answered, the nature of the cargo and the seriousness of this investigation had to be kept under the tightest wraps. There was obviously more than one person involved, and if this was not a horrendous mistake, they dared not tip the hand of whoever else might be involved. Shaun had given George all the documents he had obtained.

George was going through the notes and documents he had acquired when his intercom light came on. "Yes?"

"Trevor Johnson said he'd meet you in the executive cafeteria at noon if that's okay," said his secretary.

"Tell him that's fine. And thank you."

At noon, when George entered the cafeteria, he saw that Trevor had already arrived and secured a table in an area where they would be able to talk undisturbed. He walked over to the table to leave his briefcase while he got his lunch.

George was glad to have Trevor working with him. He could always count on him to provide good suggestions and conduct thorough research. Trevor had a knack for not getting bogged down with tunnel vision, but was able to see the big picture and was not afraid to ask the hard questions. George and Trevor had attended the same law school, though George had been a couple of years ahead. Trevor had graduated at the head of his class just as George had. They were about the same height; George outweighed Trevor but by fewer than ten pounds. They had both been jocks in high school but serious students in college and law school.

Trevor had married his college sweetheart, Grace. She had a medical degree and had opened a general practice with a friend from medical school. They put off having children while they were establishing their careers. "Children will come later," they both said.

"I take it this is about the Kingman situation," said Trevor as they ate. "I guessed that things would heat up fast after it hit the newspapers and the media made it their evening punch line."

"You guessed correctly. Do we know who leaked that to the press?"

"Not that I'm aware of, but I haven't been involved in finding that out," said Trevor. "I doubt it matters at this point, but if I were to guess, my money would be on that new kid in the mail room. That's the only thing I don't like about having interns working there. They see something that the general public doesn't know about and become all puffed up with self-importance. That's not true of the majority, but unfortunately, there's no way of screening out that one who slips in before something like this happens."

"I have an idea to run by you," said George. "As you know, once a situation has gone public, as this one certainly has, people who might otherwise talk with us clam up tight since they don't want their names on the six o'clock news."

"True," said Trevor.

"What would you think of hiring a private investigator of our own? We'd have to run whoever it is through a security screening and background check of course."

"Are you serious?" asked Trevor.

"Yes I am. Think about it. We could make up a fictional person that he or she is working for, such as a disgruntled employee who claims to have been shorted on travel expenses or something. We'd say that when all this came out in the paper, the person got scared and hired a private investigator to make sure that he or she wasn't being set up in retaliation for making a complaint against the corporation."

"Not a bad idea," said Trevor. "You seem to have given this a lot of thought. Would I be correct in assuming that you have an investigator in mind?"

"You would. I met this young woman through a friend of mine several months ago and was impressed with her ideas. I recently met her again and had a chance to discuss not only her opinions on various matters but also how she had arrived at those opinions. She gave some examples of cases she'd actually investigated—no identification was given of course—and how she arrived at her conclusions and even discussed the reasons she'd turned down a case. I was impressed."

"I think the fact that she's a woman would be to our advantage," said Trevor. "People are less likely to suspect a woman of gathering data in a case that could involve international espionage. The first thing we need to do is to get the approval of the oversight committee to hire an investigator. If and when that's cleared, you can offer her the job, and assuming she accepts, you can get the clearance process started."

"Hopefully, that will go quickly," said George. "Next, I will arrange for her to meet with the committee to give them the opportunity to ask any questions."

"Sounds good," said Trevor. "If she's as good as you say, they should have no problem approving her. They're as anxious as we are to bring this investigation to closure as quickly as possible."

"Great," said George. "I'll raise the question of hiring an investigator with the committee at tomorrow's meeting. Assuming they approve, I'll ask Jordan to dinner tomorrow night and discuss it with her. I feel sure she'll accept. When the subject of the Kingman news report came up Saturday night, she indicated that because of the numerous possibilities involved, resolving it would take some serious investigating skills, but when it was completed, the investigator would be able to feel pride in a job well done. You don't hear that type of comment very often."

"I'll say you don't. Are you sure that was for real and she wasn't just trying to impress you?" asked Trevor.

"She had no reason to impress me," said George. "I was there as a friend of Carl and Beverly, not as a Senate investigator. My job never came into the discussion."

"I may be getting a little ahead of myself, but I think that we should give some thought to sending someone to Seattle, where the cargo was supposed to go. We can't discount the possibility that someone on that end was involved. We need copies of all their paperwork, but I don't want to ask them to send it and chance getting something that's been altered."

"Good point," said Trevor. "I can probably manage that when we get to that point in the investigation."

George returned to the office to study his notes. He realized that he had not let either Boris or Shaun know where or when he was planning to meet with Boris. He checked his calendar and saw that Wednesday morning was free.

He pressed the intercom button. "Please reserve the conference room for my meeting with Boris Urich at ten thirty Wednesday morning. Then please call Boris and advise him of the time and place of the meeting. Also, call Shaun O'Riley just to let him know when and where I'll be meeting with Boris. Thank you."

Moments later, the light on his intercom went on. "The room is yours," she said.

Chapter 7

On Tuesday morning, George placed the outline that he'd prepared for his meeting with the oversight committee in his briefcase. He checked his watch. It was just past nine thirty. His meeting was at ten o'clock.

Stopping briefly at his secretary's desk, he said, "I'm heading over to the committee meeting. I probably won't be back until after lunch."

As George was approaching the conference room, he noticed Senator Granger at the water fountain a few doors down. George considered himself fortunate to be working directly for Senator Granger.

Jonathan Granger had been a senator for the past twelve years and was both loved and respected by his constituents in California because of his ability to move important issues through to completion without getting bogged down in bureaucratic red tape. That ability had served him well as a key member of the oversight committee. He was also one of the seemingly few members of Congress who were known for their personal and professional ethics in a positive way. The senator was a little over six feet tall with brown hair that was beginning to show a little gray at the temples. His features were strong and when he looked you in the eye, you just seemed to know that he was a man of his word.

As he approached, George said "Good morning Senator."

"Good morning George. I trust you have a strategy ready to present to the committee."

"Yes sir, I believe I do. Trevor and I have been working to find a way to handle this investigation in spite of all the media coverage that's been going on."

"I've been wondering about that myself," said Senator Granger. "The timing couldn't have been worse."

"I agree. That's why I'll be suggesting that we add a private investigator to our team, and I'd be grateful for your assistance in getting that approved by the committee. Trevor and I both feel that someone new and unknown might help to put the people we'll need to contact at ease and not afraid of ending up as the latest media headline."

"That's an interesting idea. I think you may be on to something. I'll back you completely with the committee," said the senator. "Let's go in now. It's time to get started."

After the preliminaries were completed, the committee chairman brought up the Kingman Corporation situation for discussion. Everyone knew that George was leading the investigation on this and he was called upon to bring the members up to date as to where things stood with the investigation. George summarized what little they had thus far and presented his plan of hiring a private investigator and his reasons for this action.

"I propose that we hire a private investigator to work with Trevor and me. I think that some of the people we'll need to interview will be more at ease speaking with someone they haven't seen on the news or read about in the newspapers. Since Shaun O'Riley was the one who brought this issue to our attention, I feel sure he'll be willing to provide an office for the investigator and furnish whatever records that we may require."

Senator Granger spoke up. "I'm completely onboard with this approach and recommend its approval."

At that point, a vote was taken on George's suggestion and received unanimous approval. George presented Jordan's name to the committee, stating that she would be required to go through the standard clearance process and that a credible scenario would be established to explain her presence.

When he had finished, the committee approved her selection and agreed that there was no need for her to appear before them prior to being hired.

When the meeting concluded, George contacted Trevor before returning to his office and advised him of the results.

"I'll go back to the office and call our investigator," said George. "By the way, her name is Jordan Anderson."

As he headed back to his office, George took out Jordan's business card. He thought back to his meeting with Shaun and Tom and the response Tom had given him when he asked why Boris's name had replaced Chester's as the Disbursement Officer just before things went wrong. His gut was telling him that there was more to this case than met the eye and he should be sure to take nothing for granted. He was looking forward to working with Jordan for more reasons than one, and seriously hoped that she wasn't involved in another case right now and was free to take on this investigation.

CHAPTER 8

J ordan had been studying the information in the copy of the side-by-side report that Sasha had prepared for Shaun. It appeared that there had been several occasions in the past when Chester's and Boris's paths had crossed. They had both attended the same college for a brief period of time, although Chester was two years ahead of Boris.

About five years later, Chester was heading up the shipping department for an international freight company. Boris worked there for about a year before leaving under questionable circumstances. According to a hand-written note in his personnel file, it was rumored that someone had accused him of altering freight manifests. Nothing could be proven, and he had voluntarily resigned, so there was no official notation made concerning the accusation in his file. The company had decided not to pass on the allegation to anyone requesting his employment history.

When Boris came to work at Kingman Corporation, it was in a shipping warehouse in Philadelphia. The report said that he had worked hard and had taken all the training courses available so he could advance. He had been well liked by his coworkers and supervisors, so when he requested a transfer due to a family emergency, it was given without question.

Jordan was about to take a break and fix a cup of tea when the telephone rang. "Hello,"

"Hello, Jordan. This is George. Did I catch you at a bad time?"

"No, not at all. I was just about to fix a cup of tea. What can I do for you?"

"I've been thinking a lot about our conversation the other night, and I'd love to take you to dinner tonight if you're free to continue our discussion. There's something that I'd like to get your opinion on."

"That's very flattering," she said. "As a matter of fact, I'm free this evening, and I'd love to have dinner with you. What time should I be ready?"

"How does seven o'clock sound to you? I have a nice seafood restaurant in mind if that's all right with you."

"Sounds perfect. I love seafood."

"Great. See you at seven. Good-bye."

George walked up to Jordan's door promptly at seven and rang the bell.

"Hi," he said as she opened the door. "Ready for some great seafood?"

"Hi yourself! Yes, I'm more than ready. After your phone call, I've had trouble thinking about anything else. That can be rough when you're trying to concentrate."

"I hope you weren't trying to concentrate on anything too important," he said with a grin.

"No. Luckily, no innocent client will suffer due to your sabotaging my thinking process." She laughed. "I'll get my purse and we can go."

The restaurant was located on the bank of the Occoquan River. The parking lot was rapidly filling up when they arrived.

They lucked out when a car pulled out of a spot right in front of the door just as they drove up.

Two couples were ahead of them, but it was not more than five minutes before the hostess led them to a crescent-shaped booth located well off the main aisle. The booth's back was high enough to provide them some privacy from other restaurant patrons. A soft light hung just above the table that added to the allure yet gave off enough light to easily read the menu.

"How about starting with a glass of chardonnay?" he asked as they placed their orders for dinner.

"That sounds perfect," Jordan replied.

The wine was served along with a basket of their famous cheddar bay biscuits, hot out of the oven. Jordan took a sip of wine and leaned back against the soft cushioned booth.

"You look very relaxed," said George.

"I am," she replied. "This is a beautiful restaurant, especially with the view of the water out this window and the soft music being played over the loudspeaker. The wine adds just the right touch. Of course, having good company doesn't hurt either. I'm glad you invited me tonight."

"I'm glad you were able to come on such short notice, and I agree with your assessment of this place. I like to come here after a hectic week. I find it very peaceful."

Their dinner was served and, as they ate, they enjoyed getting to know each other. They discovered that they had many things in common. They both enjoyed semi-classical music but did not care for hard rock. They enjoyed movies, musicals, sitcoms, biographies, and adventure stories. They also both enjoyed not only watching, but participating in sports; football and bowling seemed to be the favorites. George talked about how he and Carl were in the same bowling league and some of the amusing things that had happened during their games.

When they hit a lull in their conversation, George noticed Jordan was studying him.

"This may sound like a strange thing to say," Jordan began, "but being with you has been a pleasant surprise."

George's face registered his surprise. "Thank you … I think."

"I'm usually not this relaxed when I'm with someone new, but I feel very comfortable talking with you. I remember thinking that you were very nice when we first met at Carl and Beverly's party, and I had a good time the other evening at the movie. This time is different since it's just the two of us, but I feel very at ease, like the feeling you get when you put on a comfortable pair of slippers."

"Can't say I've ever been compared to a pair of slippers," George said, laughing. "But it sounds like that's a good thing."

"It is.," she assured him.

After finishing their meal, neither of them wanted dessert, so they just ordered coffee.

Finally, Jordan looked at him and said "George, you mentioned on the phone that there was something you wanted my opinion on. Were you serious?"

"Yes, very serious. I was most impressed with some of the things you said about how you operate your business."

"Thank you, but I don't get the connection."

"I don't know how much you know about what I do for a living."

"Beverly mentioned that you worked for a senator on the Hill, so I assume that you're politically involved."

"Well, that's true to a point," he said. "I work for Senator Jonathan Granger. He heads up a Senate oversight committee that looks into wrongdoing that involves government agencies.

I'm a Senate investigator, and very much like you, when we hear about things showing up where they weren't supposed to or of merchandise being received that no one has a record of, we get suspicious. It's my job to investigate what's going on, especially when the merchandise involved belongs to or is connected with a government agency."

"I'm impressed," said Jordan. "I had no idea that you were an investigator."

George saw Jordan's expression change like a lightbulb that had just been turned on.

"Now I understand. You're involved with finding out what happened with Kingman Corporation, aren't you? I noticed that your expression changed when I mentioned the newspaper article and Beverly mentioned the news broadcast about the cargo showing up in Afghanistan. I thought you were just interested like the rest of us. Even though the announcer made a joke out of it, it's really a big deal, isn't it?"

"Yes. A very big deal."

"Surely that's not what you want to get my opinion on," Jordan said. "How can I even have an opinion?"

"I've been checking around about you for a reason," said George. An oversight committee has authorized me to offer you a job as an investigator on this case. You'll work closely with me. If you're interested, which I seem to remember hearing you say that you were the other evening, we'll create an investigation that, to everyone else, you've been hired to solve. However, you'll actually be investigating various people at or connected with the Kingman Corporation to help us find out who was involved. We want to learn how they were able to divert a shipment, who was the intended recipient of the shipment, and what they planned to do with the missing cargo. Since this has hit the media, time is of the essence. I know you have a thousand questions, but does this sound like something you'd be interested in taking on?"

Jordan just sat there staring at George. Her eyes seemed to glaze over.

"You're serious, aren't you?" she finally managed to get out. "What could someone like me possibly bring to the table that you don't already have experienced people to handle?"

"That's a very good question," said George. "We're still not sure how this information was leaked to the press and, at this point, it really doesn't matter that much. However, since this has now gone public, anyone who might previously have been willing to speak with us will now be reluctant to talk for fear of having their name turn up on the eleven o'clock news. The idea is to set you up with a fake client, say, an employee who claims to have been shorted some expense-account money. When all of this came out in the newspaper and on the news, the employee got scared and hired a private investigator to make sure he or she wasn't being set up in retaliation for filing a complaint against the corporation."

"You make me feel like James Bond," said Jordan. "Do you really think people would talk to me?"

"Yes I do. You're not a high-profile investigator or a member of a large firm. You're listed in the phone book as an individual private investigator. You have a small office, and at the risk of sounding chauvinistic, you're female. Luckily for us, your business isn't the type or size that most people would associate with handling government matters. It's only because of our conversations that you've been approved for this job. When you were talking the other night about your criteria for accepting jobs and the ethics you apply to your work, I knew you'd be ideal for this assignment. So what do you say?"

"I say yes, I'd be honored to work with you on this investigation. I'll certainly do my best to live up to your expectations. Thank you." said Jordan.

"I don't have any exact figures at this moment, but I assure you you'll be well paid," George said. "How soon will your schedule allow you to begin?"

"Right away. I just completed my last case a couple of days ago, so I'm ready when you are."

"Great," said George. "We can begin tomorrow. The first thing you'll need to do is go through the clearance process. I'll get that set up. I'll let you know tomorrow when and where to report. Do you know Shaun O'Riley?"

"Not personally," said Jordan. "I think I've heard his name before. Isn't he connected with Kingman Corporation in some way?"

"He's the director of operations there, and he's a good man. He's working with us on this investigation. I'll let him know you'll be working with us. You can go to him for any records you want. I'm sure you'll find him to be very helpful. He'll also be told about your fake investigation, so you won't have to be concerned about watching what you say to him unless other people are around. Do you have any problem with that?"

"No," said Jordan, "no problem."

Jordan knew that she would have to talk with Sasha. At this point, she couldn't let George know that she was already well into the case, and she had to decide if she could let Sasha know that she was being hired by the oversight committee and would be working with Sasha's boss on the investigation. She had some serious thinking to do and some decisions to make. Jordan felt rather than saw that George was looking at her. She glanced at her watch and noted that it was past eleven o'clock. "I didn't realize that it had gotten so late. It looks like I'll have a busy day tomorrow, so I think we should probably go."

"I agree. I have some meetings tomorrow morning, but when I call you tomorrow afternoon about going through the clearance process, we can start planning our strategy."

"In the meanwhile, I'll set up a file on my fake investigation and prepare some notes and preliminary statements obtained from my 'fake' employee client," she said with a smile.

George paid the bill, and they left the restaurant.

When George walked Jordan to her door, he looked deep into her eyes. "I'm pleased that you decided to accept this assignment. I'm looking forward to working with you."

George gave her a light kiss on the cheek and returned to his car, leaving Jordan to wonder if she should read anything into that.

But Jordan couldn't think about that now. She had an investigation to prepare for.

Chapter 9

George got to the office Wednesday morning and had his secretary get Trevor on the phone for him.

"Trevor, can you break away for about half an hour for coffee?"

"Sure," Trevor replied. I'll meet you in the cafeteria in ten minutes."

George was sitting at the table with his cup of coffee when he saw Trevor coming toward him with coffee and a donut in hand.

They exchanged handshakes and greetings.

"From the look of you, I assume the dinner and discussion last night went well."

"You assume correctly," said George. "She's already setting up a fake investigation file with interview statements and records on her fake client. It's those little details she does automatically that make her a good investigator.

I told her that I'd be letting Shaun know about her role and that she was working with us and should receive full access to any files. She said that she was fine with that, but I thought I saw a slight hesitation when I mentioned Shaun's name. She said she had heard of him but didn't know him personally. Maybe I was just tired."

"Watch Shaun closely when you mention Jordan's name and see if he appears to have any reaction," Trevor said.

"I have a meeting at ten o'clock with Boris. He's bringing me copies of all the letters, purchase orders, and shipping documents connected with the Seattle shipment. He thinks I'll just be looking at them and making some notes, but I've arranged to have a copy machine there. It will be just outside the meeting room, and I have someone ready to handle the copying while Boris and I are talking."

"Do you really suspect that he's involved in this?" asked Trevor.

"At this point, I'm not sure, but I'm not ruling anything out. This thing about Chester suddenly dying of a heart attack when he hadn't had so much as a common cold and no history of heart problems whatever along with the fact that Boris just happened to have recently transferred to this warehouse with all of the required training and clearances doesn't sit well with me. I don't believe in coincidences. Maybe it's all legitimate, but I'm going to thoroughly check it out before I accept it at face value.

When I've finished the meeting with Boris and get back to the office, I'll set up a lunch meeting with Shaun. I want to fill him in about hiring Jordan. When we get together, I'll watch his expression to see if her name causes any reaction."

"What reason will she give Shaun for conducting this fake investigation?" asked Trevor. "Shaun has a secretary who might be listening in."

"We're using the one you and I discussed earlier. Of course Shaun will know her investigation is a fabrication. I'll mention that to Jordan when we talk this afternoon."

"By the way," said Trevor, "are you going to say anything to Shaun about your meeting with Boris?"

"Only to say that we've met and that I copied the documents Boris brought with him. I need to read over them myself before I try to discuss them with anybody."

"Good point," said Trevor. "Good luck."

George was in the conference room when Boris arrived at ten o'clock. He was about five feet, eight inches tall and looked like he had missed a few meals, although his arms were muscular from having spent several years doing warehouse work, first in Philadelphia and then in Arlington. He had what appeared to be the makings of a beard. It was longer than if he had just not shaved that morning, but the growth didn't look like it had been cleaned or combed in a couple of days. He was wearing the standard tan shirt and pants, and they were reasonably clean. His shoes showed the wear and tear that comes from being on one's feet all day.

George noted that Boris hesitated slightly as he passed the copy machine on his way into the room. "Good morning Boris," he said. "I don't think we've been formally introduced. My name is George Kilburn. You can call me George."

"Good morning," said Boris. "Here are the documents Mr. O'Riley said you'd want to look at." He handed George a folder full of papers.

"Thank you. I'm just going to have the young woman outside make copies of these and then you can take them back. That way, I'll have time to study them and you won't be left without the information should you need it. If I have any questions as I go through them, I'll call you."

George took the folder and handed it to the clerk. "While she's doing that, I'd appreciate it if you would just talk me through the procedure you followed to process the shipment from here to Seattle. Then, as I go through the documents, I'll better understand the purpose for each one."

It didn't take long for Boris to walk George verbally through each step, beginning with the initial requisition identifying the needed items and continuing through each step of the procedure until the cargo was packed and shipped.

"A large portion of the cargo consisted of routine supplies that were used regularly and special parts and equipment that were kept on hand in case of an emergency or if there was a system breakdown," Boris told him. "In addition, the shipment that was going to Seattle also contained several parcels of classified cargo that hadn't been requested by them. Each of the parcels was identified only by classified code on the shipping manifest. This is the standard procedure for sending such classified material."

By the time Boris and George finished their discussion, the clerk had completed copying the documents in the folder and had the originals ready to be returned to Boris. The copies went to George. With the copies and the notes he had taken while talking with Boris, George returned to his office and placed a call to Shaun.

"Hello, Shaun. This is George Kilburn. Have I caught you at a bad time?"

"Not at all," said Shaun. "What can I do for you?"

"I have something I need to discuss with you. Do you have any plans for lunch?"

"No, I'm free today," said Shaun. "Where do you have in mind?"

"How about Padrino's? If you like Italian, their food is about the best around; at least in my opinion."

"Padrino's is great with me. I love Italian. I'll see you there at one o'clock."

Shaun had been working in his office behind closed doors all morning. He was actually looking forward to lunch with George. He felt he needed a change of scenery. The idea of a good Italian meal was appealing as well.

At the restaurant, they ordered a bottle of red wine with their lunch.

"So what was it that you wanted to discuss with me?" asked Shaun.

"Yesterday, I met with the oversight committee and presented my strategy for conducting this investigation. It was unanimously approved."

George explained his plan to hire a private investigator to work with them on the case and what he expected to gain by such a move.

"That's great," said Shaun. "Have you decided on the investigator yet?"

"Yes, actually. We've hired an investigator named Jordan Anderson. Ever heard of her?"

"Jordan Anderson," repeated Shaun. "No. Can't say I have. You said 'her.' This private investigator is a woman?"

"Yes," said George. "Is that a problem?"

"A problem, no," said Shaun. "It's just that I'd never think of a lone woman investigator working on a case that might end up involving international espionage."

"Exactly," said George. "That's why we feel people will be willing to talk with her. You don't need to worry about allowing her to see your books. She'll have to pass all our clearance procedures first. I know her and I can assure you her ethics are second to none."

"Very well then. That works for me," said Shaun. "By the way, George, how did your meeting with Boris go? Did he give you everything you asked for?"

"Yes," said George. "He was very helpful. I made copies of all of the documents so that I can study them back at the office or home at night. I told him that if I came across anything I didn't understand, I'd call him."

"Good," said Shaun. "When can I meet our investigator?"

"Probably in a day or two, after her security check. Then, we'll be by to meet you."

By that time, they had finished lunch. George motioned for the waitress to bring the check. "This one's on me," he said as he handed her his credit card. "I'll be in touch."

The men shook hands and returned to their offices.

CHAPTER 10

J ordan was at her desk poring over the copies of the notes and the side-by-side report that Sasha had given her. Now that she was an official investigator on the case, or would be as soon as she got her security clearance, she would soon not feel like she was doing anything wrong or making Sasha do something wrong by looking at documents that she had absolutely no right to see.

Doing things she shouldn't, even when it was for the right reason, didn't sit well with her. She didn't think it would sit well with George either, so she made sure that everything Sasha had given her would remain locked in her desk drawer at home. She planned to shred the documents Sasha had given her as soon as she was officially given the documents.

Knowing that Sasha's concerns for what was going on at work would be honestly investigated and dealt with gave Jordan a good feeling. She surprised herself when she realized just how much this situation had affected her. Jordan had decided to talk to Sasha and let her know what was going on, at least the part about her becoming an aboveboard investigator and working with George. She also wanted Sasha to know that her instincts concerning

Shaun had been right on target and that Shaun was indeed one of the good guys.

George had told her that he would get her started in the security clearance process that afternoon. She estimated that she had a good three hours before he would call, so she dialed Sasha at work.

Someone else picked up the phone and said that Sasha was not in the office today but was expected back tomorrow.

Jordan was finally able to reach Sasha at home.

"Hello, Sasha, this is Jordan. You're not ill, I hope."

"No, I'm fine, thanks. I just had to take Stephanie, my four-and-a-half-year-old, to the doctor for an allergy shot. What's up?"

"We need to talk."

"Is anything wrong?"

"No. Actually, things are going better than I'd dared to hope. Would you mind if I come over? There are some things you need to know before you return to work."

"Okay," said Sasha. "I'll brew a pot of coffee."

"Sounds good. I'll be there shortly."

When Jordan arrived at Sasha's, she saw an adult-sized swing suspended by two long chains at one end of the front porch and two child-sized rocking chairs, one of which held a doll that looked well-loved and played with. A wooden railing enclosed the porch, and a hanging basket was in full bloom with flowers cascading down the sides, suspended from the ceiling. When she had driven up, Jordan could see a swing set with a slide attached in the enclosed backyard.

Jordan rang the bell, and Sasha answered it. "Hi! Come in. We can talk in the kitchen."

Sasha led Jordan to a large, bright-yellow, eat-in kitchen with lots of cabinets, an electric stove and oven, with a microwave sitting on a shelf just above it. A white, double-door refrigerator sat against the wall.

"Before I start," said Jordan, "I must ask you to give me your word that this conversation will remain confidential between the two of us."

"Yes of course," said Sasha with a curious expression on her face. "I won't say a word to anyone."

"You'll be told at work at least part of what I'm going to tell you, but you must act as if it's all news to you when you're told. If you remember, I told you that I was going to dinner with George."

"Yes. How'd that go?"

Jordan told Sasha about George's being an investigator with the Senate oversight committee and how they were investigating the situation concerning the cargo shipment. She said that they had hired her to work with him on the investigation. She told Sasha about Shaun's part in this and that he was also going to be working with them and how Sasha's instincts concerning Shaun had been right on target. She emphasized that when she met Jordan at the office, she had to act as if it were their first meeting.

"I just had to let you know all this," Jordan said. "Also, due to this turn of events, you will obviously not be billed for anything. I'm being well compensated.

I need to go now. George is going to get me started in the security clearance process this afternoon, so I need to be there to receive his call. I guess I'll be seeing you at work. Bye for now."

Jordan returned home to wait for George to call. She found that she was actually getting excited about this new adventure she was about to embark on. If truth be told, she was also getting excited about the prospect of working with George, as well.

CHAPTER 11

After lunch with Shaun, George went back to his office. He took out his notes and the copies of documents that he had received from Boris. Before he began studying them, he pressed the intercom button and asked his secretary to come in. "We've hired a private investigator to work with us on the Kingman Corporation situation," he said. "She's been approved by the oversight committee, but she needs to go through the standard security clearance process. Find out if security can do this tomorrow. Tell them it's top priority and we need this as soon as possible. If they need anything else, have them call me."

George spent the next couple of hours going over the documents, making notes and trying to figure out how the shipment could have gone astray. The documents appeared to have been handled correctly, and the procedures seemed to have been followed, but something was eluding him, and that was driving him nuts.

He stopped only when his secretary buzzed him on the intercom. "The security process will begin tomorrow morning. Jordan should report to the security office at nine o'clock. They said that the first phase should be completed by early afternoon."

George thanked her and called Jordan's number.

"Hello."

"Hello, Jordan. We're set to start the security clearance process if you can report there at nine o'clock tomorrow morning."

"Wonderful! I can be there at nine. No problem."

"I'd like to go over some things with you today if you're available. Since it's going on five o'clock now, how about having dinner with me? I can fill you in on what we have so far and what I want you to start with."

"Sure. Dinner would be fine. What time should I be ready?"

"How does seven o'clock work for you? You like Chinese, don't you?"

"Seven is fine, and I love Chinese," she said.

"Great. I'll see you at seven."

George was impressed with Jordan's eagerness to start the assignment. He knew that she was aware of the long hours of hard work they had ahead of them, but he felt she was ready for it. It wasn't until he hung up the phone that he realized he was smiling and it wasn't all because of Jordan's willingness to work. He was looking forward to dinner with her.

Jordan was ready when George arrived at seven.

"Hi," he said. "How are you at handling chopsticks?"

"I used to be pretty good at it," she said. "I guess we'll find out. You know, I can't believe how fast everything's been happening. I always heard that government was so full of red tape that it took forever to get anything done. Just a few days ago, I'd finished my last case and was wondering when something else might come up, and now, I'm in the middle of the biggest case I've ever been involved in and am about to receive government security clearance. I never dreamed that I'd ever be involved in a case that required that."

Jordan saw that George was trying to hide a laugh. She figured he thought she was babbling, and maybe she was, but when she was excited, she showed it because she could feel it in every part of her being. She believed that was what being an investigator was all about.

"I love seeing you this excited," he said. "You know that we have a lot of hard work ahead of us. Even though we're working under time restraints because of all this hitting the media, don't let the pressure get to you. I intend to do a thorough job and cover all the possibilities. If that takes extra time, that's just the way it'll be. We must be able to fully document and support our findings. The stakes are too high for us to do anything less."

"I like the way you think, George Kilburn. I know that even with all the hard work, which I don't mind in the least, I'm going to enjoy this assignment very much."

They arrived at the restaurant and were shown to their table. While they were eating, George asked how Jordan had gotten to know Beverly. She told him about how they had been best friends in college and some of the humorous situations they had gotten into as sorority sisters. After they finished eating, the dishes were cleared except for their teacups. George ordered a fresh pot of tea.

"They tell me that the preliminary portion of the clearance process should be completed by around one o'clock tomorrow," he told Jordan. "You'll get a number of documents to fill out. Then there will be a verbal interview with the department head, which will be recorded. The next step will be to have your picture taken for your identification badge. Finally, you'll get fingerprinted.

When all of that has been completed, we'll meet for lunch, and I'll give you some of the documents I've collected and introduce you to Shaun O'Riley. He's making an office available for your use while you obtain whatever additional documents you need. Any questions so far?"

"You said that everything you just went over constituted the preliminary portion of the clearance process," said Jordan. "What comes next?"

"On your application form, you'll be asked for personal and business references," said George. "You'll also be asked about your education and training. The remaining part of the process consists of members of the clearance staff checking out the information that you'll have given.

I know that this seems like overkill, but it's necessary. Everyone on the Hill with a security clearance has gone through this procedure. Don't worry. I have every confidence you'll pass with flying colors."

"When you said you believed in being thorough, you meant it," said Jordan. "I must say that I'm very impressed, and I'm anxious to get started."

"Great," said George. "You have the address and room number where you will report at nine o'clock don't you?"

"Yes, I do."

"Then I guess we're all set," said George. "Just get a good night's sleep and let the adventure begin," he said with a broad grin. He paid the bill, and they headed for the car.

When they arrived at Jordan's home, she hesitated before getting out of the car.

"Is anything wrong?" he asked.

"No, nothing's wrong. I just want to tell you that I appreciate this assignment and your confidence in me. I'm looking forward to working with you, and I'll do my best to live up to your expectations."

"That's one thing that I have no doubts about," said George as he helped her out of the car and walked her to her front door. "They'll call me when you're finished with everything. I'll pick you up for lunch. Afterward, you'll meet Shaun, and he'll get you started. Here are some papers for you to start reading. I've given Shaun a list of some of the documents you'll need to see, and he'll have those ready for you. I'm looking forward to working with you as well."

For a moment, they looked deep into each other's eyes.

"Good night, George," she said. She knew that she should open the door and go in, but she was unable to look away. The way he was looking at her held her spellbound. She knew he was going to kiss her. She also knew that was what she wanted him to do. He placed his hands on either side of her face and brought his lips down to capture hers. His kiss was very gentle but awakened every nerve in her body. Before she realized it, her arms were around his neck and she was leaning into him, not wanting the moment to end. When it did end, she was grateful that her back was against the door. She wasn't sure her legs were steady enough to keep her upright. She noticed that his breathing seemed a bit unsteady as well.

"Good night, Jordan." he said as he turned and headed for his car. That kiss was not something he had planned. It had just seemed right at the moment. He also realized he would have to maintain a professional relationship with her while they were working on this case, but he found himself humming along with the radio on the way home and thinking about how very pleasant that kiss was.

CHAPTER 12

Jordan glanced at her watch as she entered the personnel office at five minutes to nine. The woman at the desk looked up. "You must be Jordan Anderson," she said.

"Yes I am."

"I expect you were told that there would be a number of forms to fill out," the woman said. "You may use that desk by the window. My name is Charlotte Graham. If you have any questions or need anything, please don't hesitate to ask."

"Thank you. I'll keep that in mind," said Jordan.

Jordan walked to the desk thinking how much she appreciated the courtesy and helpfulness the receptionist had displayed. She then took a seat at the desk and began filling out the paperwork. She looked through the various forms and realized that obtaining a security clearance was serious business. It seemed like the only thing that she was not asked was what she had for breakfast that morning. But she hadn't gone through all the papers yet.

After Jordan had been writing for about an hour, Charlotte came over to the desk.. She looked to be about fifty or sixty; she had gray hair worn on top of her head in a bun. She wore a blue, calf-length dress and low-heeled shoes.

"Would you like some coffee?" she asked. "We have a break room right across the hall. There's a never-ending coffee pot, hot water for tea, and a soda machine. Also, the ladies room is just past the break room on the right."

"Thank you," said Jordan. "I'd love a cup of coffee."

While they enjoyed their coffee in the break room, Jordan noticed several people coming in, getting their beverages, and going back to their offices.

"Have you been working her for a long time?" she asked Charlotte.

"Yes," she replied. "I've been here for almost thirty years. I began working here right out of business school.

"You must really enjoy your work."

"I enjoy my work, but, more than that, I enjoy the people I work with and for," said Charlotte. "I can't imagine working anyplace else."

"I can tell that," replied Jordan with a smile.

After about ten minutes, the two women returned to their desks.

When Jordan had completed the last form, she took them to Charlotte. "Do I give these to you?" she asked.

"Yes," said Charlotte. "And you have perfect timing," she said with a smile. "I just got a call to take you for fingerprinting. After that, you'll have your picture taken for your identification badge and be interviewed by one of the supervisors. They'll bring you back here when that's completed."

"Great," said Jordan. "Just let me grab my purse."

The fingerprinting took only a few minutes. Following that, she was taken to another room to have a photograph taken for her identification badge. She had only a short wait until she was escorted into the office of one of the supervisors. As she entered, he stood, extended his hand, and introduced himself as Jacob Warner. He was a tall, thin man with sandy-colored hair, brown eyes, and a nice smile.

"Welcome aboard," he said. This won't take long, and I promise to make it as painless as possible," he said with a smile.

"Thank you," said Jordan. "Actually, everyone that I've met so far has gone out of their way to make me feel welcome."

"Good," said Jacob. "That's what we like to hear. I've gone over some of the paperwork you filled out. I must admit that it's not very often that I find a woman private investigator. What made you decide to enter this line of work?"

"Actually, I guess it runs in the family," said Jordan. She told him about her older brother, James, who is a JAG lawyer with the navy, and her uncle, who had been a detective with the Baltimore police department until he was killed on the job. The idea of gathering clues and reasoning out the 'how' and 'why' a crime took place and 'by whom' has always fascinated me. I've found that sometimes, things that look cut and dried are anything but and that the obvious suspect is often not the guilty person at all."

"You have an interesting approach to this business," said Jacob. "I can see why George wanted to have you brought onboard with this investigation."

They talked for another forty-five minutes or so, covering Jordan's training and education, her outside interests and hobbies, her family and friends, and any clubs or organizations she had been a member of. Finally, Jacob indicated that he was finished with his questions and asked if there was anything that she wanted to ask or say. Jordan said she had no questions and appreciated the courtesy she had been shown throughout the process.

She was escorted back to the room where she had started with Charlotte Graham.

"Well, how did it go?" asked Charlotte. "You seem to still be in one piece."

"This has been an interesting experience," said Jordan, "and I've learned a lot."

"I've let Mr. Kilburn know you've completed everything here. He said he'd be by to pick you up in about twenty minutes," said Charlotte.

CHAPTER 13

While she waited for George, Jordan went to the ladies' room to wash the remaining ink from her fingers. After being fingerprinted, Jordan had been given a cloth moistened with a special fluid to remove the ink from her hands. It had gotten most of the ink, but she didn't feel like her hands were clean. After a minute or two with some soap and hot water, she felt much better. She freshened her makeup and returned to her desk. Just after she returned, she saw George step out of the elevator and head toward her. She picked up her purse and thanked Charlotte again for her assistance. She and George headed for lunch.

"Well," George began, "how has your adventure into the wonderful world of obtaining a security clearance gone so far?"

"Great," said Jordan.

"Jacob Warner was very impressed with you. He suggested to me that we might want to consider keeping you on full-time after this investigation is completed; assuming, of course, that you don't make some egregious blunder," he said with a smile. "I don't mind telling you that Jacob is not easily impressed."

"He was very nice," said Jordan. "I just hope I can live up to his level of praise."

"You're doing just fine," said George. "I thought that we could go to The Hungry Bull for lunch if that's all right with you. They have great burgers and a well-stocked salad bar. They're used to their clients being in a hurry, so the service is always excellent."

"Sounds good to me," said Jordan.

After they had gotten their meals and found a booth, George said that they didn't need to rush with lunch. Jordan's meeting with Shaun wasn't for another hour.

While they were eating, Jordan looked around at the bulls' horns decorating the walls and the mechanical bull in the middle of the room. She noticed that there were three young men that looked like they were around eighteen or so who kept egging each other on to ride the bull. Finally, one of them did. He lasted about five seconds before he was on the floor. His buddies laughed at him. She wondered how long George would last on that thing. The image in her mind of him on the bull made her smile.

Just then, George glanced her way. "Penny for your thoughts."

"I was just picturing you on that mechanical bull," she said, smiling.

"How'd I do?"

"Trust me," she said. "You don't want to know."

That made them both laugh.

"There is one more thing that you need to know," said George.

Jordan saw that he was looking serious, so she listened patiently for him to continue.

"You know that having that cargo end up in Afghanistan is serious business," he began, watching as she nodded her head in the affirmative.

"What you haven't been told until now is the actual contents of the cargo. I didn't want to tell you until you'd completed your security clearance and were an official member of the team. Now it's time for you to know." George explained in detail the nature of the cargo and the consequences that could be expected if it got into the wrong hands.

When he finished, the look on Jordan's face told him that she understood the gravity of the task they had undertaken.

"Do you have any questions?" George asked.

"Not at this time. I knew that this was serious business, but I hadn't realized just how serious. Thanks for telling me. I'll give you my best effort. You can count on that."

"I know you will," said George.

As the hour drew to a close, they gathered their papers, George paid the check, and they left the restaurant for their meeting with Shaun.

Jordan had not spoken with Sasha for several days and didn't know what reason if any she had been given about why Jordan was coming to the office today. She hoped Sasha was a good actress and didn't let on that she already knew Jordan. She would know soon enough.

When they opened the door to Shaun's outer office, Sasha was not there. The door to Shaun's private office was open; he was working at his desk. He looked up when he heard them enter. "Come on in," he called out. "My secretary is running an errand for me and will be right back." As they entered Shaun's office, he motioned for them to take a seat at his conference table.

"You must be Jordan Anderson," said Shaun as he walked toward her with his hand extended. "I'm Shaun O'Riley, and I'm very pleased to meet you. With your assistance, I hope we can get this matter cleared up in short order. There's an office right next door that we've designated for your use. My secretary, Sasha Goldman, has been instructed to provide you with whatever you need in terms of office supplies, copying documents, or setting up interviews."

"Thank you," said Jordan. "That's very nice of you. Does Ms. Goldman know who I am and why I'm here?"

"Yes," said Shaun. "If she is to be of any help to you, it's only fair that she knows the real reason for your presence. I can assure you she can be trusted not to give you away. I have a habit of recording all meetings I attend, and Sasha transcribes them and files them. I'm involved in so many things that if I didn't keep a written record, I'd be lost. She may even remember some things that I've forgotten. If you have any questions that Sasha can't answer or if you need to discuss something, please feel free to come to me."

"I'll keep that in mind. I wish I received this kind of cooperation on all the cases I work on," Jordan said with a smile. "I'll certainly do my best to help bring this to closure as quickly as possible. However, I won't compromise my work for the sake of meeting a deadline. This will take what it takes. George has already informed me that all our findings in this case must be backed up with hard evidence. The stakes are too high to leave any stone unturned."

"I couldn't agree more," said Shaun. "As Bogie once said, 'This could be the start of a beautiful friendship.' It's no wonder George suggested you for this job."

The door to the outer office opened, and Sasha entered with a tray with three mugs of coffee. She set them on the conference table along with cream and sugar and some napkins.

"Sasha," said Shawn, "this is Jordan Anderson. You already know George Kilburn. Jordan will be working in the office next door. I've already explained that you will be available for whatever she needs."

"Hello," said Sasha. "I'm very happy to meet you, Ms. Anderson."

"Hello, Sasha," said Jordan. "I'm glad to meet you as well. I look forward to working with you, but please call me Jordan."

"Sasha has already pulled a number of documents that should be helpful to begin with," said Shaun. "I believe she's put them on the desk you'll be using."

"Thank you," said Jordan. "It sounds like it's time for me to get to work."

"I've given Jordan the documents that I received from Boris," said George. "For the most part, they should match up with documents she receives from you."

"Maybe," said Shaun. "After the meeting you and I had with Tom Clancy, I had Sasha pull Boris's and Chester's personnel files and prepare a side-by-side report on the two of them. There were some things that had been mentioned in that meeting about how Boris just happened to be available when Chester suddenly died that did not feel right. I think you'll find that document particularly interesting."

"If Sasha can show me where to go, I believe that I should get started," said Jordan.

"Take your coffee mug with you," said Shaun. "There's always a fresh pot brewing around here, so don't be shy."

Jordan gathered her things together and followed Sasha to the office next door. As she put her things on the desk, she smiled at Sasha. "This couldn't have gone any better if we had orchestrated it. From now on, my initial meeting with you happened today. There's no need to ever refer to our previous contacts. Your case is now officially cancelled. I just want to say that I appreciate your fiancé's suggestion that you contact me. Please give him my thanks."

CHAPTER 14

Jordan decided that the best place for her to start was with the side-by-side report that Sasha had prepared about Chester and Boris. Apparently, Shaun felt that he had reason to take a very close look at Boris. Since she was already familiar with the report, having received it at a previous meeting with Sasha, she set that aside for the moment and searched through the folder of papers that George had given her from his meeting with Boris. Finding what she was looking for, she took that along with the side-by-side report and moved everything else to the side of her desk.

She first read George's notes from his interview with Boris carefully. Every so often, she would stop reading and pick up the side-by-side report. She was looking for to see if what was recorded in one place was verified or contradicted by the other. Sometimes, what she was looking for was not included in the other document at all. That, too, was noteworthy. When she had found what she was looking for in the report, she made notes on her worksheet. This process was repeated over and over again. She was so focused on what she was doing that she didn't hear the door to her office open or see that George had entered.

"Knock, knock," said George when she didn't look up.

His voice startled her.

"Jordan, I'm sorry if I surprised you. I didn't realize you were so deeply into what you were reading."

It took her a minute to gather her thoughts together and then she smiled at him. "Hi. I guess I should have warned you that when I'm working on a case, I tend to block everything else out. I'm back. How are things on your end?"

"Fine," said George. "I've been in conference calls with Kingman employees in Afghanistan all afternoon."

"I didn't know that Kingman had people in Afghanistan," said Jordan. "Are they all Kingman employees, or are there also military personnel?"

"Actually, there are both. Kingman does have a skeleton crew there. Occasionally, cargo is sent to the navy personnel stationed there. Since Kingman is a private contractor, they have to keep a couple of people on location to receive and record what comes in and goes out. I've just learned that a new person was recently hired to handle the paperwork. Needless to say, he's now being very carefully watched, but at this point, there's no reason to do anything that might make anyone there suspicious. For all anyone but the top person there knows, the mis-sent cargo was all a mistake that has now been corrected. I may end up having to go to Afghanistan before this is over. How has your day gone?"

"Fast," replied Jordan. "Once I got started with these documents, I lost all track of time. Right now, I'm comparing the side-by-side report for Boris and Chester with your interview of Boris. In the morning, I plan to have Sasha obtain Chester's personnel file."

"Sounds like you're onto something," said George. "Care to share?"

"At this point, all I have is a suspicious mind and a gnawing feeling in my gut. I need to fill in some blanks before I draw any conclusions."

"Well," said George, "it's almost six o'clock and everyone else is getting ready to call it a day. I think we had better close up shop as well. How about joining me for dinner? We can go over what we have so far."

"Is it six o'clock already?" asked Jordan. "I had no idea it was that late. I'm going to take some of this home with me to go over. To answer your question, sure, dinner sounds good. It won't take me but a minute to pack up here. Shaun gave me a key to this office so that I don't have to worry about anyone seeing any papers on my desk."

Jordan stopped by Sasha's desk on her way out. "I wanted to let you know that I am leaving and will see you in the morning. I'd appreciate it if you would contact personnel in the morning and obtain everything they have concerning Chester Rafferty. Good night, and have a good evening."

"I'll be glad to," said Sasha. "By the way, here's a key card Mr. O'Riley left for you. It gives you access to the underground parking lot so you don't have to worry about finding parking on the street or pay for parking in a lot. Good night, and I hope you both have a good evening too. See you in the morning."

"Why don't you park in the underground lot, George?" Jordan asked on their way out. She remembered that George had seemed very pleased at finding a parking space on the street in front of the building.

"Actually, I do have a key card, but since I don't come here that often, I don't always carry it. I'll put it in my wallet when I get home tonight. Why don't you ride with me? I'll bring you back to your car after dinner," said George. "What are you in a mood to eat?"

"I noticed that there's an Italian restaurant just down the street," she said. "I'm told that they have good pizza. We could just walk there from here if that suits you."

"Fine with me," said George. "I love pizza. They also have a great salad bar."

"My car is parked just across the street. Let me put my briefcase in the trunk and we can head over to the restaurant," Jordan said. Once that was done, they headed down the street toward the restaurant. "It's a nice evening for a walk," she said.

They only had a few minutes to wait for a booth. They ordered a large pizza and a pitcher of beer and headed to the salad bar. "This is very nice," Jordan said, and George agreed. He was not just talking about the restaurant.

While they were eating, George said, "You were very engrossed in what you were reading when I got to your office. Did you come across something that was of particular interest?"

"Yes, I think so. From what I've seen thus far, I don't believe it was a coincidence that Boris just happened to be in this particular location with all the necessary paperwork when Chester died. I'll know more when Sasha gets me Chester's personnel file tomorrow, but something just doesn't feel right. I get the feeling that those two have a long history between them and it's not all positive, either. I think Shaun is suspicious of Boris too. If you remember during our initial meeting with Shaun, you mentioned you'd given me the documents that you'd received from Boris and that, for the most part, they should match up with documents I received from Shaun. He had a strange look on his face and replied 'Maybe,' and then he said that the fact that Boris just happened to be available with all the necessary credentials when Chester suddenly died didn't feel right to him."

"Now that you mention it, I do remember his saying that. I was going to ask him what he meant by that, but I got distracted. You may well be onto something," said George. "Good catch. I'll be interested to see what you find."

After they finished eating, they walked to where Jordan had parked her car. As she got her car keys out of her purse. George took her hand in his and said, "I'm glad you're working this case with me, Jordan, and it's not just because you're a top-notch investigator. The more time we spend together, the harder it is when we part. I probably shouldn't be telling you this now. We have to maintain a purely professional relationship while we're working on this case, but I'm beginning to like you … a lot."

The smile Jordan gave him could have illuminated a dark room like it was bathed in sunshine. "I'm very happy to hear you say that because I feel the same way about you. I also agree with you that we have to put our feelings for each other on hold until this case is completed. There's too much at stake here for either of us to become distracted. I'll admit it's something I look forward to investigating in the future."

With that, Jordan tilted her head back as George lowered his mouth to hers. His kiss began as gentle as a summer breeze, and then, as she leaned into him, his arms were around her, pulling her closer. When they broke apart, they were breathing heavily.

"I better let you go while I still can," he said. "I'll see you in the morning." He opened her door and helped her inside. He leaned through the window and gave her one more kiss before he left.

Jordan watched him walk away, still feeling the infinite tenderness with which he had kissed her. *What a day!* she thought to herself, *what a day!* She headed home knowing that she was going to have to work very hard to keep her concentration on the case, but knowing that he felt the same way she did and that this was temporary until the investigation ended would make it much easier. As they had agreed, there was too much at stake to do anything else.

CHAPTER 15

B ack at home, Jordan changed into a pair of jeans and a sweatshirt. While Jordan was sitting on the edge of the bed, Annie strolled into the room and jumped up on to the bed beside her. For the past five years, Annie had been the love of Jordan's life. She was definitely family.

As she nuzzled Jordan's hand with her head, she gave a soft meow and a look that said Jordan had been gone long enough. It was her turn to be petted and scratched behind the ears and given treats … lots of treats.

"Did you miss me, girl?" asked Jordan as she lovingly petted her. The purrs she received in reply answered her question. Jordan took Annie's comb from the table saying "Is this something that you might like?" Being combed was something that Annie loved almost as much as her treats. She reached over and laid a paw on Jordan's hand as if saying "less talk and more combing, please." As Jordan was combing Annie, she thought about the time she had spent with George. "He's quite wonderful," she said to Annie. "You'll like him when you meet him."

Jordan suddenly stopped combing. It just occurred to her that she had no idea how George felt, if anything, about animals, cats in particular. She couldn't believe that the subject had never come up. "Well, Annie, if he has a problem with cats, he'll just have to get over it or get over me. I could never be with any man who couldn't love you as much as I do."

She decided to talk to him about that tomorrow. *No,* she thought. *It can't wait that long.* She hopped off the bed, leaving Annie to wonder what had gotten into her. She headed into the living room to the phone. She had a card George had given her with his number. She picked up the receiver and dialed his home number.

George answered on the second ring. "Hello?"

"George, this is Jordan. How do you feel about animals? Do you like cats? Do you have any allergy involving cats?" she asked.

"Jordan?" he stammered. "Do I what? Cats? What're you talking about?"

"I have to know. Just answer the question please." she said.

"Yes, I love animals. Yes, I like cats. No, I don't have any cat allergies." he said. "Now, what in the name of heaven has gotten into you?"

"I have a cat," said Jordan. "Her name is Annie and she is an extremely important part of my life. I could never have a relationship with anybody who couldn't love her as much as I do. You must come over here for dinner one evening so you two can meet. Are you agreeable to that?"

George figured that laughing would not have been the wisest reaction at that point, although maintaining a calm voice was one of the hardest things he had ever done under the circumstances. "Yes," he said in as serious a voice as he could. "I'd be very pleased to have dinner with you and Annie. Just tell me where and when, and I'll be there. I hope you won't mind if I don't have bells on, though. I draw a line in the sandbox over bells. Is there anything else you want to know?"

"No, that's all I need to know for now," said Jordan. "I'll let you know when to come for dinner. Just so you know, I'm glad you like cats. Good night, George."

She hung up the phone. She didn't care if George was wondering if she had been sniffing catnip instead of Annie.

Having gotten that matter settled to her satisfaction, Jordan went to her desk and took out the notes she had made about the side-by-side report.

There was a two-year difference in Chester's and Boris's ages, but, for two semesters, they had both attended the same junior college.

After college, Boris had been employed to work in the shipping department of the same international freight company where Chester was the shipping department manager. Boris later resigned under questionable circumstances that had something to do with altering freight manifests.

Chester began work at Kingman as the disbursement officer in the Arlington warehouse. Boris began working at Kingman in the shipping warehouse located in Philadelphia. The file indicated that he had taken and passed every course he could to qualify for a disbursement officer position himself. When it looked like he was about to be selected for a management position, he requested a transfer to the warehouse in Arlington. Even though it meant that he would be in a position that paid the same as he was being paid in his current job, he stated that he had a family emergency and needed to live closer to them. He was transferred with the promise of a promotion to management as soon as a position became available. There was nothing in his file that disclosed the nature of the emergency or what family member was in need.

Jordan read Boris's personnel file. He had been born in the United States shortly after his parents had come through Ellis

Island from Russia. Boris had a brother who was three when his parents came to America. He had died years later of pneumonia. Boris had been truthful about his education as far as he went, but he had failed to include that he had taken several courses related to medicine. According to the file, Boris had wanted to be a doctor when he was young and had even taken some medical courses relating to diagnostics. The courses were very general and covered information about different kinds of diseases, how one might catch the diseases, the symptoms each might present with, and what types of medicines might be used to treat them. He never went further in the medical field due to bad grades. He took some courses in other fields but finally just dropped out of college altogether.

Jordan glanced at her watch and realized that it was getting late. She knew she had a busy day ahead of her and needed to be able to remain alert. Although she had only had two glasses of beer with dinner, she felt that the best thing she could do now was feed Annie and get a good night's rest. After putting the dish of food on Annie's dinner mat and filling her bowl with fresh, cool water, Jordan turned out the lights and went to bed.

As she settled down, Jordan's thoughts were not about the case and the questions that she needed answered. They were of George and his kiss and how wonderful she had felt when he had taken her in his arms and told her he was falling for her. She drifted off to sleep with a smile.

CHAPTER 16

When she got to the office the next morning, Jordan was happily surprised to find the personnel folder for Chester on her desk. She was just about to get herself a cup of coffee when Sasha walked into her office carrying a freshly washed mug filled with fresh, hot coffee.

"Good morning," said Sasha. "I thought you could probably use this."

"Good morning to you," said Jordan. "You're a mind reader. While I appreciate this, please don't think that I expect you to bring me coffee every morning."

"It's no problem," said Sasha. "I make the coffee when I get in each morning, and if others are in, I usually bring them some."

"By the way, Sasha, thank you for getting that file for me so quickly."

"Just let me know if you need anything else," said Sasha as she left to return to her desk.

Jordan placed Boris's personnel folder on her desk to her left. She placed the side-by-side report in the center. She put the copies of the documents Boris had given George and George's notes on them to her right. Each time she picked up a document from his personnel folder, she found the entry covering the same information in the side-by-side report. She took the document covering that information from the stack on her right, if it existed. She compared the three to see if the content did or didn't match. It was a slow process but the only way she knew to discover any discrepancies.

The initial information dealing with his name, address, telephone number, where and when he attended college, and where and when he was subsequently employed were basically the same. However, only his personnel file mentioned the fact that his parents had immigrated to the United States from Russia just before he was born or that he had an older brother who had been born in Russia and had died from pneumonia as an adult in the United States. Jordan listed this information on her notepad.

The fact that Boris had once considered a career in the medical profession and had taken several medical courses relating to diagnosing diseases, symptoms, and treatments was also mentioned only in his personnel file. This information, also, was added to Jordan's note pad.

Only his personnel file had mentioned that when he worked at an international freight company, the job he held just before starting with Kingman in Philadelphia, he had left voluntarily but under questionable circumstances. There was nothing that mentioned exactly what those circumstances were. There was also nothing mentioned in any document to explain the nature of the family emergency that had resulted in his wanting to transfer from Philadelphia to Arlington.

The omission of these pieces of information in itself did not constitute a reason to believe that he was guilty of anything. It was, however, curious, and in Jordan's mind, it raised questions that needed answers.

The buzz of her intercom and the blinking light on the outside line indicated that she had an incoming call.

"Hello, this is Jordan Anderson."

"Hello, Jordan, this is George. How are things going?"

"Hello, George. Slowly but steadily." She told him how she was proceeding through Boris's personnel file. "I've come up with several questions but no answers to them yet. When you have time, I'd like to go over them with you."

"I was just stopping for lunch," George said. "Why don't I pick you up out front and we can discuss what you have over lunch."

"That sounds good," said Jordan. "Give me ten minutes and I'll be outside."

Jordan put her notepad in her briefcase and stopped by Sasha's desk long enough to let her know that she was meeting George for a lunch meeting. She wanted to leave the stacks on her desk in the order she had put them in, so she locked her door as she left. She had just walked out the front door when she saw George drive up. She got in the front seat and they headed for lunch.

"There's a place just a few minutes south of here," he said, "where they have a good salad bar and almost any kind of soup or sandwich you could want. I like that they also have booths so we can talk without being overheard."

"Sounds great," Jordan said.

"I'm very impressed with the way you're going about this," said George. "I know that it's slow going, but your method makes sure that nothing is missed. Have you spoken with Shaun about any of this yet?"

"No I haven't. I want to finish going through the personnel file and my notes before I meet with Shaun. I believe some of the things I'm finding should have been caught before now. I can only assume at this point that Chester's sudden death caused things that would normally have been done thoroughly and carefully to move at a much faster pace in order to get the position filled. It's possible that someone planned this to happen in just that way. I don't have proof of that, but I think when some of these questions are answered, we'll have all the proof we need."

They arrived at the restaurant and were shown to a booth. The food was served cafeteria style and the waitress just came by to refill drink containers and to clean the table when a party left. They got soup, salad, iced tea, and frozen yogurt for dessert.

After they had finished eating, Jordan took out her notepad and went over the items she had found that appeared only in Boris's personnel file. "I suspect that Boris may not even be aware that this information is on record anywhere," she said. "I feel fairly sure that when applicants complete the paperwork required when they apply for a position, if nothing looks suspicious, they're hired. The personnel staff would follow up on the application later by contacting former employers and references and maybe even contacting colleges or universities that were listed as being attended. As that information trickles in, it's probably looked over to see if anything stands out. If nothing does, there'd be no reason for anyone to pull the file and compare that information against the information provided by the applicant."

"You make an excellent point," said George. "In the majority of cases, doing that kind of comparison would be a waste of time because, for most people, the data would match up."

"I think we're going to need to conduct some interviews ourselves," said Jordan. "I suggest we contact the junior college that he attended and the international freight company where he worked prior to working for Kingman in Philadelphia. I'd like to know exactly what those questionable circumstances that caused him to resign were. The file stated that his older brother died of pneumonia. I'd expect that since they had come from Russia, the family would live close to each other and very possibly have the same doctor. I'd like to know if there were any other health issues in the family.

"Maybe there's a reason Boris didn't continue with his interest in medicine other than just bad grades. When people go to college with particular fields in mind, they may not make the honor role, but they don't usually flunk out either unless something has made them not want to continue studying in that field."

"Why don't you take the junior college? I'll take the international freight company," said George. "We can say that Boris is being considered for a high-security government position as the reason for our inquiry. I'm sure the oversight committee will have no objection to that under the circumstances. We can also do a genealogy search on the Internet."

"I'll ask Sasha to do the internet search," Jordan said. "She's computer savvy and can probably do that with no problem. I'll put her on that when I get back to the office."

"I know that you said you wanted to wait until you've finished going through the personnel file, but I think we should meet with Shaun today," said George, "especially since we're now planning to involve Sasha in the search process."

"You're right," said Jordan. "I heard him tell Sasha he'd be in meetings this morning but would be in the office in the afternoon. I'll call Sasha now and see if he's back or when he's expected."

Jordan called on her cell phone and found that Shaun was at lunch but would be back within the next few minutes. Sasha said she would let him know that they would be in to see him shortly. They talked for a few more minutes before they gathered their things, paid their bill, and headed back to meet with Shaun.

CHAPTER 17

When George and Jordan entered the office, Sasha told them to go right into Shaun's office as he was expecting them. As they walked in, Shaun stood and motioned for them to sit at his conference table. George began the conversation. "We wanted to meet with you because Jordan has found some things that have raised several questions. We'll want Sasha to do some searching on the Internet and we just wanted to keep you up to speed with what we're doing."

Jordan filled Shaun in on how she was conducting her search. She said that she had found certain information in Boris's personnel file but nowhere else and that she had some guesses as to why and how that had occurred. She mentioned the questions that had arisen in her mind as a result. Shaun listened carefully.

"I plan to contact the junior college, and George is going to contact the international freight company," she said. "George seems sure the oversight committee won't have any problem with our stating that the reason for our inquiry is that Boris is being considered for a high-security government position and allowing them to believe this is standard operating procedure for this level job. I plan to have Sasha do an Internet genealogy search and see if that turns up any information."

"I'm impressed," said Shaun. "I'm in full agreement with everything you've said. George, you remember the day of our first meeting with Tom. You asked about seeing Chester's and then Boris's name listed as the disbursement officer and wondered why the signature had changed. When I went through the time line of events concerning Chester's death and Boris's replacing him, I was shocked. Until I laid it out like that, I hadn't questioned how it had been such fortuitous luck that Boris was onboard and available to just step into that position with all of the security clearances in place. If you hadn't asked, I would never have had Sasha do that side-by-side report, and I certainly wouldn't have considered the fact that personnel records may contain information that the applicant didn't know existed."

"I'll meet with Sasha about the genealogy search now," said Jordan. "I'll also have her write out the name and address of the international freight company and the phone number of the head of personnel," she said, directing the comment to George. "You can pick it up on your way out." With that, Jordan stepped out of the office to speak with Sasha.

"I don't know how you happened to come across Jordan," said Shaun, "but we're lucky that you did. She's one of the most intelligent investigators that I've ever met. If I were you, I'd make every attempt to hang on to her and offer her a permanent position."

"I couldn't agree more," said George.

Jordan was heading toward Sasha's desk when she noticed that she was on the phone. Sasha looked up as Jordan got nearer and saw her motion to come into her office when she finished on the phone.

A few minutes later, Sasha came into Jordan's office. "You wanted to see me?"

"Yes," said Jordan. "Are you familiar with how to conduct a genealogy search on the internet?"

"Sure," replied Sasha. "I've been tracing my family's genealogy for the past two years. What do you need?"

"Boris's personnel records indicate that his parents were Russian immigrants who came to the US just prior to Boris's birth. They also indicate that he had a brother three years older than him. The brother was said to have died of pneumonia when he was an adult. No specific age was given concerning his death. Boris hadn't furnished any of this information since he began employment with Kingman Corporation. I need you to find out everything that you can about his family. You don't need to trace further back than his grandparents.

"His records also indicate that at one time he was interested in medicine and had begun taking courses toward obtaining a medical degree. See if there's any mention of his brother's illness. Was it really pneumonia that he died from? I'm following up with the school that he attended to see how serious he was about studying medicine. I want to know what courses he took, did he make passing grades, and why he abandoned it. As you're doing your search, please keep an eye open for anything that would have a bearing on his medical training or of any unusual illnesses occurring in his family. Any questions?"

"Not at this time," said Sasha. "This seems pretty straightforward."

"Good," said Jordan. "Don't hesitate to interrupt me if anything appears strange to you."

"I'll start right away. I know that this is a serious case, but doing this genealogy search is something that I enjoy."

"Oh by the way," said Jordan, "please write out the name and address of the international freight company where Boris worked just prior to coming to work with Kingman in Philadelphia. George will be stopping by for it on his way out. He also needs the name and phone number of their head of personnel."

"I'll do that first," Sasha said.

Jordan then turned her attention to tracking down the address and phone number of the school Boris had attended. She tried to remember if she had seen it listed in any of the notes that were included in the personnel file. A thorough search of the file revealed nothing. She would have to find another way. Until an idea came to her, she would continue reviewing the personnel files.

So far, the review of Chester's personnel file had been consistent with information that he had furnished. One document caused Jordan to do a double take. Buried in the file, Jordan had come across a report that the medical examiner's office had furnished several weeks after Chester's death. The report stated that an autopsy had been performed that revealed traces of a deadly toxic substance in the blood. The sole source of this substance is the venom of a snake that was found only in a remote region in India. Since the death certificate on Rafferty had already been filed listing the cause of death as a massive heart attack, apparently nobody knew what to do with this report and it had just been filed away and forgotten.

Jordan went online to search for information about the substance. She found that anyone coming in contact with this substance would be rendered helpless immediately and would be dead within about thirty seconds. She learned that the reaction to the venom could seem like a heart attack. Jordan made a copy of the medical examiner's report. She also printed out a copy of her findings from the internet search. She realized that a huge question had arisen. *Did Chester die from a heart attack, or had he somehow been poisoned.* That would seem to be the only way this deadly substance would gain entry into his system, but how would anyone in Virginia gain access to, or even find out about, rare snake venom from a remote region of India; clear across the world?

Jordan looked further into Chester's file and found the name and telephone number of his primary care physician, Dr. John Cannon, which Chester furnished when he obtained his security clearance. She called the doctor and identified herself. She explained her reason for calling was that she was looking into granting security clearance for the person who had replaced Chester. She wanted to see if Chester had had any history of heart problems. The doctor said he would check his records and would fax her his report. Jordan thanked him and returned to her review of the records.

CHAPTER 18

Sasha learned that Boris had been employed by Higby International Freight Company located in East Orange, New Jersey, just prior to his employment with the Kingman Corporation in Philadelphia. Roger Thompson was head of personnel at Higby. She gave the information to George as he was on his way out of the office.

"Thanks," he said. "I won't bother Jordan now, but I'd appreciate it if you would just tell her that I'll be back for her at six o'clock."

"I'll make sure she knows," said Sasha. She was well underway with her genealogy search of Boris and was surprised at how much information she was able to find.

A while later, Jordan came out of her office and asked Sasha, "Have you had much luck locating anything on Boris?"

"Surprisingly yes," replied Sasha. "He did have an older brother, Omar, who died from pneumonia at age thirty-nine. Apparently, his mother had been sick for a number of years before she was finally diagnosed as having a malignant tumor. By the time they found out what it was, the cancer had spread throughout her body. That appears to be what turned Boris toward medicine.

"I also found out that he attended Med Start Junior College located just outside Towson, Maryland. It's a private, two-year school that offers all of the basic college courses needed to enter Johns Hopkins in Baltimore. Their catalog offers some online medical courses taught by Johns Hopkins professors. Because it's a junior college, it can offer them at a lower cost than most other schools. I made a note of the name and phone number for you."

"That's great," said Jordan. "Thank you. It seems that you've had more luck with that than I did."

"Boris's mother died when he was partway through his second year at Med Start," said Sasha. "I don't know whether that broke his spirit or whether he no longer had the money to continue, but that was when he dropped out. If he and his mother were close, losing her like that would account for a drop in his grades as well."

Since Med Start was not more than an hour's drive from the office, Jordan decided to go there for the information she wanted instead of obtaining it by phone. She called the school and was connected with the dean's office. She explained who she was and set up a meeting with Professor Andrew Jorgenson, Boris's guidance counselor, for ten thirty Monday morning.

As soon as Jordan had hung up the receiver from setting up her meeting, she looked up to see saw Sasha standing just inside her doorway. "Come in, Sasha. Do you need to see me?"

"This fax just came in from Dr. John Cannon, Chester Rafferty's primary care physician."

"Great. I've been waiting for that." Sasha handed her the fax. It was seven pages long. The information appeared to be routine and covered pretty much the same things that had been disclosed in his personnel file. When she reached page four, however, she stopped reading, sat up straight, and reread the paragraph she had just finished.

The report stated that Chester had never had any heart problems and neither had any members of his family. In the years covering his adolescence, the doctor stated that Chester had contracted a serious case of asthma. It had caused him to miss enough time from school that he had to attend summer school to graduate on time. Jordan picked up Chester's personnel file and began searching through all of the papers. She knew that she remembered seeing where he had been given an EKG.

Every year, as a part of their health care package, Kingman Corporation has a medical team come to the plant and administer a variety of tests to all of their employees, which included chest X-rays, blood tests, and EKGs. They tested for high blood pressure, diabetes, glaucoma, heart problems, and hearing problems. Employees diagnosed with any such problems were encouraged to seek medical attention at no loss of pay. To obtain this free health care, the employees agreed to allow the corporation to keep copies of these records.

Jordan remembered seeing a sign stating that the corporation has a gym on location and all employees had free use of it before and after work and during lunch.

The employees, including Chester Rafferty, had just gone through their annual physical exams the week before Chester had had his heart attack. All his tests had shown him to be in excellent shape. Jordan searched through his medical file twice to see if there was any notation made or question raised as to why a man in top physical shape would suddenly drop dead from a massive heart attack, but there was nothing. She could not understand how this could have been overlooked. *Hadn't his family raised any questions? Hadn't the company doctor who had performed the physical just a week prior to his death raised any questions?*

Jordan realized that she had not seen anything that listed the name of the company doctor. She pressed the intercom button and asked Sasha if Shaun was in his office. Finding out that he was, Jordan walked over to his door and knocked.

"Come in," said Shaun.

"I'm sorry to bother you," said Jordan, "but I was wondering who the company doctor here at Kingman is."

"We don't have a doctor on staff," said Shaun. "We maintain a nurse practitioner here full-time."

"Who conducts the annual physical examinations?"

"We contract with a local physician here in the area to handle those," said Shaun. "I believe that his name is Dr. John Cannon."

"Hmmm. He's listed in Rafferty's personnel file as being his primary physician."

"Yes," said Shaun. "Being local, he's the primary physician for a number of our employees. We couldn't see where that would cause any conflict of interest. Performing the annual physicals is the only thing he does for the company. He's free to keep a copy of the annual physical report for any of his patients, but he doesn't furnish any additional patient information to us."

Jordan asked Sasha to get Dr. Cannon on the phone.

"Dr. Cannon, thank you for speaking with me again."

"What can I do for you, Ms. Anderson?"

"In regard to Chester Rafferty's death, am I correct in assuming that you assisted the medical examiner with the autopsy?"

"Yes," said Dr. Cannon. "Since I'm the doctor of record for Kingman Corporation, I was there when the medical examiner performed the autopsy. Two signatures are required, so I was there to witness the procedure. Is there a problem?"

"That's what I'm trying to determine," said Jordan. "The medical report showed traces of a deadly snake venom found in Mr. Rafferty's blood. Can you tell me if either the medical examiner or you saw any puncture marks on Mr. Rafferty's body?"

"There was a puncture mark on his neck we couldn't explain. It was just behind his right ear. I remember that the medical examiner commented on it as being strange since Mr. Rafferty hadn't been taking any medication that required a needle. At that time, he hadn't gotten the results of the blood draw back, so neither of us gave it too much thought. Are you suggesting that may be how the venom got into his blood?"

"That's the question that I'm raising, yes."

"Yes, it is possible that it could have happened that way," said Dr. Cannon. "That was the only mark we found that we couldn't explain. Under the circumstances, I think that would have to be the way the poison entered his body. Since the puncture mark was found right away and the poison wasn't discovered until the lab results were back several weeks later, neither of us thought of connecting the two."

"That's another thing that I don't understand," said Jordan. "Why did it take several weeks to get those lab results back? Blood work doesn't usually take but a day or two."

"In most cases, that's true," said Dr. Cannon. "However, this venom is rare, and it was certainly not something that any of us would have expected to have found when conducting a fairly routine blood test. I'm not at all surprised that it took that long to identify the source.

"Knowing what we know now, if I were to make an educated guess, I'd say the poison was probably put on the point of a small dart or pin. It would only take a drop of that venom to do the job. Mr. Rafferty's system was partially compromised due to the asthma he had contracted in his youth. Even if the dart hadn't punctured the skin, the poison on his skin would have been absorbed with the same result, taking only a little longer. From all outward appearances, Mr. Rafferty would have had a heart attack. What happens now?"

"That's not up to me," replied Jordan. "Thank you for your assistance."

CHAPTER 19

George went back to his office and spent part of the afternoon going over notes from the meeting he and Jordan had with Shaun. The information that Jordan had uncovered had not only proved beneficial in and of itself, it had also provided leads that would undoubtedly result in obtaining evidence crucial to the case. He heard a knock on his door. "Come in."

Trevor stuck his head around the door. "You busy?" he asked.

"Hi, Trevor," said George. "Come in. Have a seat. I was just thinking about giving you a call. Things are going well. Jordan found the name of the school Boris attended and is going to find out just how much medical training he'd received and where he was heading with it. She has Sasha doing a genealogy search on the internet to see what we might find there.

"We've found the international freight company Boris worked for just before he started with Kingman Corporation in Philadelphia. I'm planning to drive there on Monday. They're located in East Orange, New Jersey, so it shouldn't be more than a three-hour drive each way. I want to know what those mysterious circumstances were that surrounded his resignation. I was wondering if you'd like to take a trip on Monday."

"You want me to accompany you to New Jersey?" asked Trevor.

"No," said George. "I want you to fly to Seattle and talk to the people in the receiving department. Get copies of the purchase orders and shipping manifests, and try to get their side of what might have happened. It strikes me as odd that we haven't heard anything from Seattle concerning this mess. The shipping manifests that accompanied their shipment should have shown that they were not only receiving the routine cargo that they had requested but also additional cargo of a classified nature. I'd think they would have contacted us when that portion of their shipment didn't arrive, but I have yet to hear one word from them."

"That's strange," said Trevor. "Sure, I can fly out Monday morning. Is the company jet available, or should I book a commercial flight?"

"I'm sure the company jet is available." George pressed the intercom button and asked his secretary to arrange for Trevor to fly out on the jet. He also advised her that he would be driving to East Orange, New Jersey on Monday morning and would return some time in the afternoon. In a matter of minutes, she buzzed him and said that the jet would be ready for Trevor at nine o'clock Monday morning.

George filled Trevor in on all they had found thus far.

"This is going much better than we'd hoped," said Trevor. "You said that Jordan was good, but I had no idea just how good."

"I suspect that you wouldn't be upset if she was working with us every day," said Trevor with a knowing smile. "Of course, if that happened, she'd have to be assigned to someone other than you. That is, if my intuition is working on all cylinders. Couples aren't allowed to work under the same manager."

"Slow down there, Speedy Gonzalez," said George. "Who said that Jordan and I were a couple? Until we started working together on this case, I'd seen her only twice, and both of those times we were with a group. I admit that she's a woman I'd like to get to know better, but for now, our relationship is strictly platonic. It has to be."

George glanced at his watch. It was a quarter to six. "I left word that I'd pick Jordan up at six o'clock," he said. "We're going to eat and go over what we discovered today. Care to join us?"

"I'd love to, but my wife has other plans," said Trevor. "I think we're going shopping for a new washer and dryer. She said something on the phone about holding a funeral for the ones currently in use at our house."

"I'm sure that you won't get back until late Monday," said George. "Let's plan to meet around nine o'clock Tuesday and see where we stand. I'll let Jordan know."

"Will do," said Trevor. He picked up his briefcase and headed to the elevator. "Have a safe trip."

"You too," said George. He gathered his things and headed for his car to pick up Jordan.

As soon as he got in the car, George called Jordan.

"Just calling to let you know that I'm in the car and ready to leave. What about you?"

"Sasha just walked back into the office, so I'm ready to head for the elevator. Meet you out front?" she asked.

"I'll be there," he said.

Jordan picked up her purse and briefcase and, after locking her door, she headed for the elevator. She stopped long enough to say good night to Sasha and to wish her a good evening.

CHAPTER 20

Jordan was walking out the front door as George pulled up. He leaned across the seat to open the door for her.

"Hi," he said. "You look tired. Have you run into any problems?"

"Hi yourself," Jordan replied. "Actually, case wise, this has been a very good day. But it's been a very busy day, and I'm ready to relax. I think you'll be pleased when we compare notes… after dinner, if that's all right with you."

"Absolutely. How does a glass of wine and a good steak sound to you?"

"Like heaven," she replied with a smile.

A few minutes later, George pulled into the parking lot of one of the more popular steak restaurants. He had made reservations on his way to pick up Jordan. He was very glad that he had when he saw the number of people waiting to be seated. The restaurant had valet parking, so they didn't have to worry about finding a spot.

When they entered the restaurant, George gave the maître d' his name, and they were seated in a booth immediately. George told the waiter to bring them a bottle of wine right away. By the time they had gotten comfortable, the waiter was back with the wine in an ice bucket, two glasses, and a plate of crackers and cheeses.

"This is very nice," Jordan said as she leaned against the plush back of the booth. "I didn't realize that I was hungry until we got here and I smelled all these wonderful smells."

"Remind me to send Carl and Beverly a very special gift," said George. "I'm so grateful to them for introducing us."

George reached over, took Jordan's hand and leaned down to place a kiss in the center of her palm.

Jordan felt that small gesture all the way to her toes. From the expression she saw on George's face, he had felt it too. She looked in his eyes and was captivated by the warmth that seemed to radiate from his very soul. This was one time that Jordan wished she could press a button and their booth would be sealed off from the rest of the world. She had dated many men in her life, but none had ever had the effect that being with George was having on her. It wasn't just in this romantic setting either. All of a sudden, Jordan realized that George had asked her a question.

"I'm sorry. What did you ask?"

"I asked how Sasha was working out."

"She's doing a great job. She's a natural on the computer. Sasha found that Boris had attended Med Start Junior College in Maryland for just under two years and had taken some online medical courses given by professors from Johns Hopkins University. I have an appointment to meet with his guidance counselor Monday at ten thirty."

Their dinners came. They postponed further discussion of the case until they had finished eating.

After they left the restaurant, Jordan told George about the health care package Kingman offered its employees. "It's the best that I've ever come across." She briefly described the coverage, giving particular emphasis to the yearly free physicals that took place at work. "Chester was given this exam the week before he died." she said.

George had been listening while driving, but when Jordan said that, he pulled over and turned off the ignition. "Rafferty took his exam the week before he died?"

"I thought that would get your attention. It gets even more interesting. I went back through his medical file and found that all of his tests had shown him to be in excellent shape. I received a fax from Dr. John Cannon, Chester's primary care physician. He told me that neither Chester nor any of his family had ever had heart problems."

"Didn't you say that Dr. Cannon was the doctor on staff for the corporation as well as Chester's own primary care physician?"

"Yes I did. Before you ask, I raised that question with Shaun. He said that Dr. Cannon was the primary care physician for a number of employees at Kingman. When I went through Chester's personnel file, I came across a report from the medical examiner's office that had been received several weeks after Chester's death. That report stated that the autopsy revealed traces of a deadly toxic substance in his blood. The substance turned out to have come from the venom of a snake found only in a remote part of India. An Internet search told me that anyone coming in physical contact with the substance would be rendered helpless immediately and dead in about five minutes. The person would appear to have suffered a heart attack. I can only assume that since this report came in several weeks after Rafferty's death and since the death certificate had already given the cause of death as a heart attack, nobody knew what to do with the report, so it was just placed in the file.

After receiving the fax from Dr. Cannon and looking through Chester's personnel folder, I called and spoke with him again. He said that he'd been at the autopsy as a witness so he could sign the death certificate. I asked him if they'd seen any puncture marks on Chester's body. He said that there had been a puncture mark on Rafferty's neck that they couldn't explain since Rafferty was not taking any medication that required a needle. Even if he had been, no shot would have been given in the neck. He told me that the puncture mark could definitely have been the way the poison entered Chester's body.

Dr. Cannon further stated that the only reason he and the medical examiner had not come to that conclusion was because the results of the lab tests revealing the existence of the poison didn't come in for several weeks after the autopsy was performed. When I questioned the length of time the tests took, he said that because the venom was so rare, it had taken longer to identify it."

"Excellent work, Jordan. I think you've gotten enough to show that Chester was murdered instead of dying of natural causes. We just need to find out who obtained the poison, who administered it to Chester, why it was done, and how."

"I think we have enough to consider Boris a suspect at least," said Jordan.

"Agreed," said George. "Trevor and I will also be on the road Monday. He's flying to Seattle to look into Kingman records there and find out why they never reported a shortage on their last shipment. I'm going to New Jersey to meet with the owner or manager of Higby International Freight Company. I want to learn what those questionable circumstances were that surrounded Boris's resignation. We'll probably both be back too late to have a meeting Monday, so let's meet Tuesday at nine o'clock in my office. I want to go through what we've found before meeting with Shaun."

"I should be back in the office by around two o'clock Monday," said Jordan. "I'll put all this in order for Tuesday's meeting."

When they arrived at the lot where she was parked, Jordan got out of the car and, giving him a big smile, just said "Have a safe trip."

CHAPTER 21

Jordan arrived at Med Start Junior College about ten fifteen on Monday and was shown to the office of the guidance counselor. As she entered, she was greeted by a man who looked to be in his mid to late forty's. His hair looked like it had been jet black when he was younger, but now it was showing more of a salt-and-pepper grey. He was about six feet tall and had a large build but was not fat. His eyes were grey and prominent under thick eyebrows that matched his hair.

"Good morning, Ms. Anderson," he said, extending his hand in greeting. "I'm Andrew Jorgenson, and I hope you had a pleasant drive here this morning."

"Good morning, Professor Jorgenson," she said, taking his hand. "The drive was very pleasant, thank you. I appreciate your taking time to meet with me."

"How may I help you?" he inquired.

"I want to discuss a former student of yours," she began. "His name is Boris Urich. I understand that he attended here for just under two years. If you remember him, I'd appreciate knowing whatever you can tell me."

"Yes, I remember Boris. May I ask why you are inquiring about him?"

"Of course. Mr. Urich is being considered for a high-security government position, and I'm conducting a background check on him."

"Very well. Boris was a good student and showed great promise in the field of medical research. He was fascinated with rare and fatal diseases and how they were contracted. When his mother died, Boris dropped out of school, but I'm not sure if it was because of her death or if there was some other reason."

"Anything else?" asked Jordan.

"I believe that he also took some medical courses online given by several professors from Johns Hopkins University. That's about all I remember right now. Please feel free to contact me if you have any further questions."

"I will. Thank you, Professor Jorgenson," Jordan said as she picked up her things and headed for her car.

At eight thirty Monday morning, Trevor Johnson arrived at the Kingman airfield where the corporation's jet was located. With briefcase in hand, he crossed the airstrip and boarded the plane. "Good morning, Joe," said Trevor to the pilot, who was going through his preflight checklist. "What's the weather look like for the flight?"

"Good morning," Joe replied. "According to the reports, we should have a smooth ride all the way. There was talk early this morning about some rough weather when we pass over Colorado, but that storm seems to have gone farther south. I guess this is our lucky day."

"Works for me," said Trevor. "I've never enjoyed flying through storms."

"There's coffee and sandwiches in the galley. Since you're the only passenger today, they didn't send along a flight attendant. We'll just have to fend for ourselves."

"Thanks. I'll remember that," said Trevor as he turned and headed for the passenger compartment and took his seat.

"We'll be taking off in about five minutes, so be sure to buckle up," said Joe.

They made good time with little or no turbulence. When they arrived in Seattle, they were directed to an airstrip that was not used very often. Since this was a private plane, they taxied to a hanger that was owned by Kingman. As he was leaving the plane, Trevor paused at the captain's cabin and thanked Joe for the good ride. "This shouldn't take more than two, three hours," he said.

"I'll be here whenever you're ready," said Joe. "Good luck."

Trevor checked in with the person on duty inside the hanger and picked up a set of keys to the vehicle he would be using while he was here. While it was referred to as the Seattle warehouse, it was actually located in Bremerton, not far from the naval base. He drove onto the Bremerton ferry for the ride across Puget Sound. He had an option of staying in the car for the trip or going up to the deck area where he could visit the snack shop or just walk around and stretch his legs. He chose the latter. Walking out on the deck, he stood by the railing, enjoying the view and the feel of the sun on his face.

When the ferry was getting close to Bremerton, Trevor went down to his car and was ready to drive off when they docked. It was a short drive from the ferry to the naval base. He passed by a gas station, a couple of small motels and a mom and pop grocery store. Once he was on base, his route took him passed the commissary and through the base housing. There were several administrative buildings before he reached his destination.

As he entered the office, he noticed the man sitting behind the desk who stood and stretched his hand out to Trevor. "Hello," he said. "I'm Robert Jenkins, but most people call me Bob."

"Hello, Bob," said Trevor as he shook Bob's hand. "I'm Trevor Johnson. Glad to meet you."

Bob was on the short side, about five feet, four inches tall. He was well filled out, though Trevor suspected that he had more muscle than fat. He had sandy-colored hair and green eyes. He was wearing jeans and a blue sweatshirt with a chain of keys hanging from his belt.

"I'm not sure that I understand the reason for your visit," said Bob. "We haven't had any problems I'm aware of."

"Let's just say that there have been some strange things happening and I'm hoping you can help us to figure it out," said Trevor.

Bob motioned toward a table and chairs. "Let's sit here. Would you like some coffee?"

"Coffee would be great," said Trevor.

While Bob was getting the coffee, Trevor put his briefcase on the table and removed some papers and a writing pad. Once they were settled, Trevor began. "Have you had any reports of missing cargo here?"

"Not that I know of. What kind of cargo? When was it supposed to have gone missing?"

"I'll answer that in a minute," said Trevor. "First, did you hear anything on the news about some cargo turning up in Afghanistan?"

"Now that you mention it, I do remember hearing something along those lines on the radio one morning when I was coming to work," said Bob. "I didn't think much about it, though. Was that Kingman cargo, and did that really happen?"

"Unfortunately, yes. It was cargo that was supposed to have arrived here from the Arlington warehouse," said Trevor.

"What kind of cargo?"

Trevor gave Bob a description of the cargo.

"Oh my God!" said Bob. He went to his desk, pressed the intercom button, and asked his secretary to pull all the requisitions, bills of lading, and shipping manifests for the past month.

"I was aware that system was in the works," said Bob, "but I had no idea that it had been completed or that it was being included with this shipment."

"Are you saying the shipping manifest documents that accompanied this last shipment didn't list additional classified cargo you hadn't requested?" asked Trevor.

Just then, the secretary knocked on the door and entered with a stack of files. She set them on the table. "This is everything, sir," she said. She left, closing the door behind her.

"No," replied Bob as he handed Trevor the most recent shipping manifests covering cargo that they had just received. "As you can see, the shipping manifest shows only what we requisitioned. How could anything like this have happened?"

"That's what we're trying to find out," said Trevor.

"Please rest assured that we'll do anything you ask of us to help," said Bob.

"I'll need copies of these requisitions, bills of lading, and shipping manifests to take with me," said Trevor. "I won't need any other backup data."

"Of course," said Bob. He picked up the files and took them out to his secretary, giving her instructions of which documents to copy and put in a folder. "While we're waiting for the copies," he said, "let me walk you through the process."

CHAPTER 22

George was up and out early Monday morning, heading for Higby International Freight Company in East Orange, New Jersey. He had called ahead and had set up a meeting with Roger Thompson, head of personnel. He had not mentioned the reason for wanting the meeting. When George arrived, Roger was on a telephone call so he was given a cup of coffee while he waited.

After about five minutes, the door opened and a man came out. He walked toward George with his hand extended. "You must be George Kilburn. I'm Roger Thompson. Sorry to keep you waiting. Let's go into my office."

George set his cup on the table and stood to shake Roger's hand. "Your secretary took good care of me while I waited," he said with a smile.

Roger led the way and indicated a chair across from his own. "Please have a seat. What can I do for you?"

"A few years ago, you had a man named Boris Urich working in your warehouse. I understand that he voluntarily resigned but that his resignation was surrounded by mysterious circumstances. I'd like to know what those circumstances were and what kind of employee Boris Urich really was."

"May I ask why you're asking about Mr. Urich and how you'd know about any mysterious circumstances if there were any?" asked Roger.

"Of course," said George. "I work for Senator Granger and an oversight committee in Washington, D.C.," he said as he showed Roger his ID. "Mr. Urich is being considered for a high-security government position. We have to check out all previous employers and references. I'll try not to take up too much of your time."

"I understand perfectly," said Roger. "Let me get his file."

It seemed as if Roger was looking for something specific as he paged through the file. Finally, he came to the section that he had apparently been looking for.

"For the most part," Roger began, "Boris was a good employee. He caught on fast, was always on time, and carried out his duties as well as anyone could want. The only person Boris had any problem with was his supervisor."

"Who was his supervisor?"

"His name was Chester Rafferty. Chester was with us for several years and worked his way up to head of the shipping department. He was an exemplary employee. In the beginning, everything seemed fine, but as time went by, there were rumors among the employees that there was friction between them. Chester began watching Boris like a hawk.

One day, I received a call from one of our regular customers telling me that part of his order was missing; it hadn't been received. I asked Chester about it, and he showed me the requisition showing that the client had requested the items that were reported missing. He also had a copy of the shipping manifest showing that all the requested items had been in stock and were shipped. However, since this involved one of our best customers and since he swore that he hadn't receive the items in question, I authorized the missing items to be shipped again. That happened again two times. Chester questioned Boris about it, but Boris would say only that the items had been shipped."

"What kind of items were missing?" asked George. "Were they routine items, or were they special order?"

"That's just it. They were routine items; things that were periodically ordered.

"One day when Boris wasn't at work, Chester opened his locker and found copies of the three shipping manifest forms, except that those forms didn't include the missing items. In every other way, they were identical to the ones Boris had shown Chester, including the date and requisition number.

The next day, Chester asked Boris why those other forms were in his locker. He accused him of altering the forms. Boris argued that he'd never seen them before and tried to accuse Chester of setting him up. Chester had covered himself by talking to management about his suspicion and having a manager and a security guard with him when he opened the locker.

Boris knew he'd been caught. He then gave a story about how he'd been approached by some men who claimed they'd hurt him if he didn't comply with what they wanted. He said he'd had no choice. Since he had been so quick to change his story, we didn't believe him but had no way of knowing what the real truth was. After clearing it with me, Chester told Boris that if he resigned and cleared out that day, he wouldn't put what he was accused of in his personnel file. If he's up for a high-level position, I wouldn't recommend it."

George thanked Roger for the information. The secretary brought a folder of the shipping documents. "I'd like to ask that you not discuss this meeting with anyone," said George.

"I appreciate all you've disclosed and these copies. You've been extremely helpful."

"I'm glad this has helped," said Roger. "Please call me if there's anything else you need. I always regretted we didn't have enough proof to take action at the time. By the way, if you come across Chester, please give him my best. He's always welcome back here."

"I'm sorry to tell you this," said George, "but Chester died of a heart attack not too long ago."

"Heart attack?" questioned Roger. "I can't believe it. Chester was always watching what he ate. After lunch, he'd go jogging. He was very health conscious."

"That's very interesting," said George. "We're looking into the circumstances surrounding his death and feel he might have received some unwanted help in bringing it about. Do you have any medical records for Chester while he was here?"

"I believe there's something in his file. Let me check." He pulled Chester's file and found medical records that showed Chester had been in excellent shape. He made copies for George.

"Thank you again," said George as he left.

With that, he gathered his things together and headed for the parking lot. Before he started his trip, he called Jordan to let her know he was on his way home. He said he would stop by her house and fill her in on what he had discovered.

"Don't eat on your way back," she said. "I'll have something ready when you get here. You like spaghetti?"

"You bet. I'll pick up some wine to go with it."

"That sounds great. See you soon. Don't bother to knock when you get here. I'll leave the door unlocked so you can come on in."

CHAPTER 23

J ordan always kept several quart jars of homemade spaghetti sauce in the cupboard. Her recipe had been handed down from her grandmother to her mother and then to her and had won rave reviews from three generations of satisfied palates. She emptied the sauce into a pan and set it on low. She sliced a loaf of Italian bread halfway through and filled the spaces with slices of butter.

She went to her china cabinet for her special dinnerware. Her good china had a blue floral pattern around the rim of the plates and serving dishes. The set had been given to her by her mother and she treasured it. She got out her crystal wine glasses and her best silverware. She tucked cloth napkins into silver napkin rings and set a bottle opener for the wine next to the place setting where George would sit. On the table were two candles in crystal candlesticks she planned to light when they sat down to eat.

She looked around to give her place a last-minute inspection.

She turned on the oven but planned to wait to put the bread in until she heard George drive up. She busied herself making a tossed salad. George had told her he'd be stopping by his place to freshen up. He had called to let her know that he was leaving his home and would soon be there. She put the spaghetti in the boiling water. By the time he arrived, dinner would be just about ready.

When George walked in the front door, bottle of wine in hand, he caught the wonderful aromas of homemade spaghetti sauce and hot, buttered Italian bread.

"Hi!" said Jordan. "Welcome back." He held up the bottle of wine that he brought for her to see. "You'll find a corkscrew bottle opener on the table next to the glasses. Go ahead and pour the wine while I put everything on the table. I hope you're hungry."

"First things first," he said. He set the wine on the table and headed to the kitchen.

Knowing what he had in mind, she turned toward him just as his arms went around her waist.

His kiss was gentle as his mouth settled over hers, but it increased in intensity as he pulled her close. It had only been one day that they had been apart, but it had felt like an eternity to Jordan. By the time that he lifted his head and looked into her eyes, they were both breathing heavily.

The bell on the stove signaled that the bread was ready. She brought the serving dishes to the table as George poured the wine and lit the candles.

When they finished eating, Jordan filled two mugs with hot coffee, and they took them to the living room. George sat on the couch. Jordan slipped her shoes off and sat next to him with her feet curled up under her and her head leaning against his shoulder.

As if on cue, Jordan heard a soft "meow" coming from the hall.

Annie had paused in the doorway, having just realized the source of the strange sounds she had heard. She was staring at this intruder who was cutting in on her special time with Jordan.

For a moment, the way Annie was staring at him made George feel almost guilty.

It was all Jordan could do not to laugh out loud.

"Come here, Annie," said Jordan as she patted the couch cushion next to her. As Annie walked slowly toward her, Jordan said, "I want you to meet George."

As an added incentive, Jordan motioned for George to retrieve the bag of cat treats from the table next to him. The minute he picked up the bag, Annie's pace hastened considerably. She jumped up on Jordan's lap and accepted a treat from George's fingers. Once she connected George with Jordan and treats, she was ready to form a friendship. Before long, she was sitting on George's lap, purring happily and munching another treat.

A potential crisis had been averted.

Jordan turned her attention back to George. "How did your trip go?" she asked. "Were you able to find out about the questionable circumstances surrounding Boris's leaving?"

"Yes. I found out about that and more. Roger Thompson, the head of personnel at Higby International, told me that Boris had gotten along well with everyone except his supervisor."

"Let me guess," said Jordan. "Chester was his supervisor."

"Give that lady a gold star. From what Roger said, neither man had mentioned that they had known each other previously. As time went on, it became apparent to everyone that there was bad blood between the two."

George told Jordan about the customers who had complained about not receiving parts of their shipments and how Chester had discovered that Boris was apparently falsifying the records and stealing the merchandise. "Since Boris first denied it and then changed his story to say that he was threatened, they couldn't be sure of what was the real truth, so they were hesitant to prosecute.

Boris was given the option of resigning. If he agreed to resign and leave immediately, those incidents would not be recorded in his permanent record.

"When I told Roger that Chester had died of a heart attack, he was speechless. He gave me copies of Chester's medical records while he was working there. It seems Chester had a reputation for being a health nut. He was very conscientious about what he ate and would often jog after lunch."

"Things aren't looking good for Boris," said Jordan.

"No they're not," said George. "While I'm fairly certain that Chester didn't die of natural causes, we don't have any evidence to charge Boris or anyone else with his murder. We know he died from a deadly substance that was introduced into his blood, likely through a needle or a dart, but we haven't yet been able to determine who obtained the substance and how the act was carried out. I'm anxious to hear what Trevor discovered at Kingman's Seattle location today. We'll be meeting with him tomorrow morning."

George glanced at his watch. It was getting late.

As he stood, he said "Thank you for dinner, Jordan. It was great. As hard as we've been pushing on this case, it's nice to kick back and relax even if it's only for a couple of hours. Tomorrow's going to be another busy day."

Jordan took his hand and walked him to the door. He paused to tell Annie how much he had enjoyed meeting her and slipped her an extra treat. "Looks like you passed inspection," she said with a smile. "You also have excellent taste in wine."

George turned her around so that her back was against the door. He kissed her neck and gave her jawline a series of kisses, working his way to her lips. He brushed his mouth across her lips very gently several times. She felt an electric current traveling through her body. He finally locked onto her mouth. A slight moan escaped her lips as they parted to give entrance to his tongue, which probed her mouth, each thrust better than the previous. When he finally lifted his mouth from hers, Jordan found that her arms had encircled his neck. She was clinging to him, not sure if her legs would support her if she let go.

With one final kiss, he said good night and headed out the door.

Jordan stood transfixed. She watched him until his car was out of sight. From somewhere deep inside, a bright light was flashing "caution." She realized she was falling for this man and falling hard. *What if this doesn't work out between us?* She knew she needed to go to bed but doubted if she would do much sleeping.

CHAPTER 24

Jordan arrived at her office around seven thirty the next morning. George had said that she and Trevor should meet in his office at nine o'clock to go over all the documents they had gathered, lay out what they knew and could prove, and raise their unanswered questions. George wanted to make sure that they would not have any distractions while they sorted through their material. After they had everything arranged in sequential order, they would be in a better position to report their findings to date.

Jordan wanted to go over her information once more to make sure that she had not left anything out.

Sasha arrived shortly after Jordan had and was surprised to see her hard at work that early. She made coffee and brought a mug to Jordan.

"Good morning," she said. "You look like you could use this. How early did you come in?"

"Just a few minutes before you did," said Jordan. "Thanks for the coffee. You're right. I can use this. I'm just getting ready for our nine o'clock meeting."

"Anything I can do to help?"

"No," said Jordan, "but thanks for asking. I think I have everything in order. Has there been anything new in the last day or so?"

"Not that I know of," said Sasha. "Actually, things have been pretty quiet lately."

Just before nine o'clock, Jordan filled her briefcase and headed out the door. "I'm not sure how long this meeting will last," she told Sasha. "If you need me, call me on my cell phone. Otherwise, I'll call you when we break for lunch."

George had reserved a conference room. They spread everything out on a long table and pulled a whiteboard and colored markers out of a closet. George had had coffee and some Danish set up at one end of the room. He was looking through the information he had gathered when Jordan entered. By the time she had set her briefcase and purse down, Trevor had arrived. They exchanged greetings and helped themselves to the refreshments.

"I think we're ready to get started," said George. "Jordan, will you fill us in on your strategy and what you've had Sasha doing?"

"Sure. I began by going through the files and documents I got from George and Shaun." She explained how she had compared the information Boris had given George during his interview against information in his personnel file. "People tell you only what they want you to know about themselves," she said.

She explained how most people believed that personnel files contained only the information they had supplied when they applied for employment and didn't consider the fact that the employer will obtain additional information from previous employers, school records, and references the potential employees provide. "When people furnish information about someone else, they tend to tell everything they know. It raises the question of why the applicant didn't reveal some of the information others provided."

Jordan pointed out that Boris had not disclosed the fact that he had taken some medical courses at a junior college and had a fascination with, and working knowledge of, rare and fatal diseases and medical diagnostics.

"This information comes into play only because of a report that came in from the medical examiner's office stating that the autopsy blood work had disclosed the presence of a deadly and rare toxin that appeared to be the cause of his death.

The sole source of that substance is the venom of a snake found only in a remote region in India," Jordan said. "Dr. John Cannon, Chester's primary care physician, told me that he and the medical examiner had found an unexplained puncture mark on Chester's neck. When specifically asked, Dr. Cannon stated that in his professional opinion that puncture mark was probably the means by which the poison had entered Chester's body. The outward signs of this toxin mimic heart attacks.

"I believe we have proof that Chester didn't die of natural causes. He was murdered. We know Boris has lied by omission of numerous facts. The facts that we now have aren't enough to charge Boris with murder, but they do make him a suspect. We know he possessed the capability of administering the poison, and their history shows a possible motive, but we don't know how Boris could have obtained the poison."

George listed the various points that Jordan had gone over on the whiteboard in two columns; one listed the actions they could prove; the other listed questions that still required proof. "This is a good start," said George. "Trevor, would you please share what you've found?"

"Of course," said Trevor. "First, let me say you gave an impressive report, Jordan."

"Thank you," she responded.

Trevor discussed his trip to Seattle and his meeting with Robert Jenkins. He related Robert's surprise at finding out that the cargo that had landed in Afghanistan was to have gone to Seattle. The copies of the shipping manifests he had received with the shipment did not list any cargo other than what they had requisitioned. That mystery was yet to be solved.

"Good job, both of you," George said. "Now it's my turn. I went to Higby after Jordan discovered that Boris had worked there just prior to his coming to work for Kingman. I was told that in general, Boris was a good employee. He performed his duties well and got along with everyone except for his supervisor, who just happened to be Chester. He told of how several customers had been shorted merchandise from their shipments and how altered documents had been discovered in Boris's locker. Because of the way that Boris had lied initially and then, when he was caught in that lie, changed his story to say that he had been threatened, there was nothing to stop him from changing his story again. Since no one had actually seen Boris place the documents there, Chester agreed to not record this in his personnel file if Boris would resign and clear out that same day, which he did.

"From the data gathered thus far and based on what happened at Higby, it appears that when Boris received the requisition from Seattle, he knew the security system was to be added to the shipping manifest as additional classified cargo. He made a copy of the outgoing shipping manifest and deleted the classified cargo items from it. It was the duplicate shipping manifest that was actually shipped to Seattle. I suspect he destroyed or hid the original.

"It's my guess that Boris made a copy of the original requisition received from Afghanistan and added the security system to the copy. The shipping manifest was prepared based on the altered copy of the requisition, and it accompanied the cargo through the shipping department up until it was actually being shipped from the warehouse. At that time, Boris must have exchanged it for a copy of the shipping manifest that was identical except that it listed only the items originally requisitioned. The shipping manifest listing only those items that had appeared on the original requisition was the one that accompanied the shipment to Afghanistan. Boris has probably destroyed the shipping manifest that listed the security system by now.

"There has to be someone in Afghanistan working with Boris. We don't know to whom the security system was going or who was working with him in Afghanistan to remove the security system from the rest of the cargo and get it to the intended recipient. It's only by sheer luck that the shipment was received by someone other than the person Boris had intended to receive it."

"How did that happen?" asked Jordan.

"I'm not sure," said George, "but my guess is that the person who was designated to receive that shipment was either reassigned to another job or maybe was out sick. I'm going to Afghanistan to see if I can solve that portion of the puzzle. There has to be a duplicate set of the shipping manifest documents somewhere.

"In parting, Roger said that if I saw Chester, I should say hello for him. He said Chester would be welcome back at Higby any time. I told him about Chester's death. He couldn't believe it. He said Chester had been extremely health conscious. He always watched what he ate and would go jogging after lunch. He gave me copies of Chester's health records while he was at Higby."

"Chester's personnel file indicates that it was shortly after his problems with Boris at Higby that he was selected to fill the position of disbursement officer here at Kingman's Arlington location," Jordan said.

"Trevor," said George, "I'm leaving Thursday morning for Afghanistan to talk with the Kingman people there. While I'm doing that, I'd like you to go to Philly and speak with the warehouse manager there. I believe his name's Philip Croft. See what their records show about why Boris had left Higby. What position did he hold? Did he receive any special training or promotions while he was there? I believe there was something about a family emergency that resulted in his transfer to Arlington. Find out everything you can about that. Also, find out if Boris got his security clearance in Philly or after he transferred to Arlington.

"Jordan, I'd like you to go through Boris's personnel file again and see what training he received after he reported to Arlington. Is there anything to indicate whether Chester even knew Boris was working here? Were any of Boris's previous employment problems known to personnel in Arlington before he was promoted to replace Chester? Have the telephone logs for the period beginning with Boris's promotion to disbursement officer to the present pulled, and see if there were any calls made out of the country. Boris may not be aware that all telephone calls are logged and kept for ten years.

The meeting ended.

CHAPTER 25

Jordan had a good feeling as she gathered her things. The meeting had gone well. While they still didn't have the evidence they needed to prove their case, they were gathering important information, and the pieces were beginning to form a picture.

It was a few minutes to one o'clock. On his way out, George told her he had a lunch meeting he was committed to attend, but if she was free, he would pick her up at home around six thirty and they would go out to dinner.

Jordan said that she would be ready.

Remembering she had told Sasha that she would check in at lunch, Jordan called her.

"Hi, Sasha. We just finished our meeting. Want to meet me at the pizza parlor across from the office for lunch? My treat."

"Sure. I can be there in ten minutes."

"Great. Get a booth and order a large pepperoni. I'd like a house salad too, with ranch dressing and iced tea. Get whatever you want. I'm on my way."

Jordan had just arrived when the waitress brought their lunch. "Good timing," she said to Sasha. "This smells heavenly."

"How did the meeting go?" asked Sasha.

"It went very well. We've gathered a bunch of material, but we still have more to do. Some big holes need filling in, but I believe we'll have a very strong case by the time we're ready to act on it. George and Trevor have trips to make this week, and I need to go back through everything in the personnel files. I'll probably be calling on you again for your assistance. How's your workload?"

"Shaun has been keeping me busy, but I'm sure I can help with anything you need. He's made it clear that this case gets top priority."

"Great. Is he going to be in the office this afternoon?"

"Yes. He has no meetings this afternoon. Want me to set up a meeting with him?"

"I'd appreciate about five minutes of his time when we get back"

Jordan had just walked into her office and put her purse in her desk drawer when the light on her intercom came on.

"He's free now if you want to go in," said Sasha.

Jordan walked over and knocked on Shaun's door.

"Come in," he said.

"I won't take but a minute of your time, but can I get copies of the telephone logs from the date Boris was promoted to disbursement officer? I'm primarily interested in seeing if there were any calls made to or received from Afghanistan."

"Sure," said Shaun. "We have a record of any and all calls that were made from the warehouse for the past ten years. I'll have that sent to you right away."

"What about calls made from outside the warehouse? Is there any way of tracking any cell phone calls that Boris might have made?"

"We don't ask employees for their cell phone numbers unless the nature of their job requires that they be available twenty-four hours a day," said Shaun. "The position of disbursement officer wouldn't fall into that category. Also, if Boris made any such calls, I doubt that he would have used any phone that we could trace. My guess would be that, if he made any calls to Afghanistan, he'd have used a burn phone and made the calls away from here to ensure that he couldn't accidentally be overheard."

"That makes sense," said Jordan.

"At any rate, you'll have our phone logs before you leave this afternoon."

"Thanks," she said as she returned to her office.

Trevor returned to his office and stopped by his secretary's desk. "I'll be driving up to Kingman's Philadelphia plant tomorrow," he said. "Please see if Philip Croft can meet with me. He's the warehouse manager. I should arrive there around ten thirty. If that's not convenient for him, find out when he's free."

A few minutes later, his secretary buzzed him that Mr. Croft would be available to meet with him at ten thirty. Trevor settled in for the afternoon and went over his notes from the morning's meeting with Jordan and George.

He intended to find out what kind of employee Boris was during his time at the Philadelphia plant when he met with Croft the next day. Had he done only what was required, or had he been willing to do whatever needed doing? How had he gotten along with other employees and his supervisors? Did he take any courses to qualify for advancement? Why had he come to work at Kingman? What jobs had he previously held, and why had he left his job to work at Kingman? Had he obtained his security clearance requirements in Philadelphia? What was the reason for his requested transfer to the Arlington warehouse? What family member had needed his assistance and why? Trevor had a long list of questions for Philip Croft.

George went by Senator Granger's office to fill him in on the information they had gathered and how they were proceeding. After he'd gone through what each member of the team had uncovered and how the various pieces were seemingly coming together, he explained what they felt were the main questions that remained unanswered.

He said that Trevor was going to the Philadelphia plant to meet with the warehouse manager. "We need to find out what reason, if any, Boris gave for being unemployed. Had he mentioned his former employment with Higby International or why he was no longer there? Did he obtain his security clearance there or after transferring to Arlington? We want to find out the nature of the family emergency that had caused him to request a transfer to Arlington.

"While we have a number of suspicions and leads we're tracking down," George said to Senator Granger, "the only thing we know for sure at this point is that Chester hadn't died of natural causes. I'm flying to Afghanistan on Thursday to meet with the Kingman people there. I'm letting them think I'm there to retrieve the unrequested cargo they received. I hope to find out much more. We believe Boris is a key player in this scenario and that he had to be working with someone at the Afghanistan facility, but we aren't yet able to prove that."

"It sounds like you're embarking on a dangerous part of this case," said Senator Granger. "I have a man who works with the American embassy there who I want you to contact as soon as you arrive. He's well connected in the inner circles of what's going on over there and may prove to be a valuable asset. His name is Omar Kadiere. I'll let him know you'll be contacting him."

"Thank you," said George. "I welcome any help he can give. It may be a long shot, but I'm hoping to find a lead that will give us a connection to the snake venom. We don't know that it came by way of Afghanistan, but it's our best guess at this point for a place to begin looking."

Senator Granger gave George a card with Omar Kadiere's name and number. "Make sure the first place you go is the embassy. People who've made contact with the embassy are a little less of a target than those who haven't."

"I'll remember that. Thank you, Senator."

It was about four thirty when Sasha came into Jordan's office carrying a package. "This was just delivered for you," she said as she handed the package to Jordan.

"These must be the phone records," Jordan said as she removed the contents from the folder. The list was set up by date and time and recorded every telephone call, both incoming and outgoing, beginning with the day Boris began as the disbursement officer until the close of business yesterday. As Shaun had predicted, the records showed no calls being made to or received from Afghanistan. What Shaun had said about Boris using a burn phone was probably correct, she thought to herself, and, if so, there was no possibility of ever tracking that down. There was absolutely no question that this had been an extremely well thought out plan.

The next morning, Trevor began his trip to Philadelphia. When he arrived at the plant, he was directed to the office of Philip Croft, the warehouse manager. As he entered the warehouse, Trevor saw a man walking toward him.

"Good morning, Trevor. What can we do for you?"

"Good morning, Philip. I'd like to speak with you about a former employee. Is there someplace we can talk in private?"

"Of course. My office. It's right around the corner."

On the way in, Philip stopped at his secretary's desk and asked her to hold all his calls and to bring coffee. Philip motioned to the conference table in his office and asked, "What can I help you with?"

"We're looking at a former employee of yours here as a possible candidate for promotion to a security-sensitive position," Trevor said. "The employee's name is Boris Urich. I'd appreciate your telling me everything you can about what his duties were when he worked for you, what training he received, and how he handled his assignments. I'd also like to know how well he got along with management and coworkers."

"Boris Urich," said Philip. "I remember him. He worked in shipping. As I recall, he was a good guy. His coworkers seemed to get along well with him. He was always on time and completed all his work. I'm not surprised he's up for promotion. That was always on his mind while he was here."

"What do you mean?" asked Trevor.

"He was always signing up for any class or training he could. He seemed to be driven to becoming a manager." said Philip.

"Did he ever have a job that required security clearance?"

"He was about to just before he transferred to Arlington. A manager's position opened up in shipping. He applied for it and had met all of the qualifications and had even been interviewed. We were all sure he would get it and the substantial raise in pay that came with it. Just before the announcement was to be made, however, he requested a transfer to Arlington. I couldn't understand it at the time. The position he transferred into paid the same as he was being paid in his current job. I asked him why he was requesting the transfer just when he seemed about to be given a promotion to management at a much higher salary. He said he had a family situation that required him to be in the Arlington area. I think he said that he had a sick mother. His brother had gotten into some financial difficulties and wasn't able to care for her any more. You can't fault a man for wanting to care for his family."

"It's a good person who puts his family before his own needs," commented Trevor.. "Was this all included in his personnel file?"

"I'm sure it must have been. I'll have my secretary make you a copy of his file."

"Thank you. I appreciate that. I think that takes care of about everything I need. You've been very helpful, and I appreciate your taking time to meet with me."

While he was gathering his notes, the secretary came in with a copy of Boris's personnel file. Trevor thanked Philip again and headed for his car. He was anxious to read that file but knew it would be better to wait until he returned to Arlington. Trevor knew he would be too late getting back to meet with George, so he called him on his hands-free device.

CHAPTER 26

George had stopped at Jordan's house on his way home. He didn't have time to go out to dinner with her; he had to pack and get his paperwork together before leaving for Afghanistan the next morning. He picked up a bucket of chicken and mashed potatoes, coleslaw, and biscuits that they could eat while going over last-minute details. While they were eating, his cell phone rang.

"Hello," he said.

"Hello, George," said Trevor. "I just wanted to touch base before you left in the morning. I knew it would be too late by the time I got home."

"Good," said George. "How'd your meeting go?"

"We have some interesting developments," said Trevor. "I spoke with Philip Croft, the warehouse manager. He was not at all surprised when I told him Boris was under consideration for a promotion to a security position. The picture he painted of Boris was of a model employee whose career goal was to become a warehouse manager as fast as possible. Philip described him as being 'driven.'"

"That's interesting," said George. "Just wanted to let you know you're on speakerphone. I'm at Jordan's."

"No problem," said Trevor. "I hope your day went well, Jordan."

"Yes, thanks. It has. Were you able to find out what the emergency was that caused Boris to ask for that transfer to Arlington?"

"As a matter of fact, I did. You'll never guess what the emergency was. If you remember, Boris's records show that his mother and brother died some time ago. Boris gave his reason for the transfer as needing to take care of his sick mother because his brother had run into financial difficulties and was no longer able to care for her."

"You're kidding!" said George.

"No I'm not," said Trevor. "That was the reason he gave, and because he was up for promotion at the time and the transfer would constitute a lateral move, no one gave it a second thought or saw any reason to check it out. They all believed that if he was willing to give up a promotion that he'd worked so hard to get to take care of his sick mother, he must have been a saint and should be given as much assistance as they could. Also, the promotion he gave up would have given him security clearance, and I'm sure when the people in Arlington realized that, granting his security clearance went through pro forma."

"The man is smart. I'll say that for him," said Jordan. "That was a brilliant tactic. For now, I think we should just let things ride and not ask any questions. We don't want Boris thinking he's a suspect."

Both George and Trevor agreed.

."With that," said Trevor, "I bid you both good night. Have a safe trip, George. Jordan, you have my number if you need anything."

"Yes, thanks," Jordan replied. "Good night."

While George and Jordan finished eating, they discussed these new developments. Then George gathered his papers, said good night to Jordan, and went home to pack. He promised to call her the next night after he was settled in. She promised to say a prayer that he return home safely.

George was up early the next morning. Trevor had uncovered some important information in Philadelphia. Clearly, Boris was unaware that his personnel records had included the facts that his mother and brother had been deceased some time before he requested the transfer to Arlington. George knew his trip would be their only opportunity to obtain information concerning the handling of the cargo shipment that had taken place in Afghanistan.

George had been given the name of Rashi Mubarek as the person who had been on duty and had signed for the unscheduled cargo shipment. He needed the name of the person who was supposed to have been on duty when the shipment came in and the reason the change had been made without anyone suspecting he was looking for anything unusual.

This information would be crucial to the case, and how he went about getting it was as important as the information itself. If he did not come across as just a guy who was sent to pick up a shipment that had been sent by mistake, not only could they lose their one shot at obtaining the information that they needed, but his life could be in jeopardy as well.

His first call after he checked into the hotel would be to Omar Kadiere, his contact at the American embassy and friend of Senator Granger. He would make all his calls to Kadiere on his cell phone so that they could not be traced. It had been arranged that he would contact the warehouse manager, Stanley Fremont, when he was settled at the hotel. A car was coming to take him to the Kingman facility. George had been assured that he could speak freely in front of Fremont and that he could be trusted to provide him with whatever records he needed. He would, however, need to be sure that no one else overheard their conversations.

George was going over his checklist one last time when he heard a horn blowing outside. He had decided to take a taxi to the airport. When he returned, he would have the missing cargo with him and had arranged to have a van from Kingman take possession of it at the airport and give him a ride back to the office. He was sure that he could get a ride home with Jordan.

The cab made good time considering the rush-hour traffic on the beltway. He arrived at Dulles Airport with time to spare. Fortunately, he did not have a long wait to get through security. His briefcase was his only carry-on, and that passed inspection with no problem. He experienced a momentary delay when he forgot to remove his keys from his pocket, which set off an alarm. As soon as he realized what he had done and removed the keys, he was cleared and sent on his way to the boarding area. He had a first-class seat, which allowed him room to open his briefcase and make notes. He liked the amenities that first class, passengers received, especially on long flights, as this one certainly was. Even though it was a direct flight, so he didn't have to worry about changing planes or long layovers, he was looking at about fifteen hours, give or take, of travel time.

Once they had taken off, the flight attendants welcomed the passengers and went over the usual flight instructions concerning the use of seat belts, oxygen masks, and so on. They also pointed out the restrooms and emergency exits and cautioned passengers to check the screen just above their heads before getting out of their seats to see if the captain had turned on the "fasten seat belt" sign.

A few minutes later, after the flight attendant had come by with beverages and snacks, George looked around at his fellow passengers. He enjoyed mentally deciding whether they were traveling on business or for pleasure. A person traveling alone might be a business executive on his way to close some important deal or a student who had been studying abroad and was returning home. A family might be returning from a vacation or be in the military en route to a new location. On long trips, this helped to pass the time.

It was several hours into the flight when George lowered his tray table and opened his briefcase. He took out a large notepad, a pen, and notes he'd made when he had last met with Jordan and Trevor. He began making a list of things they knew and questions that still needed answers.

Boris either caused or was involved in the death of Chester.

Chester had not died of a heart attack, but had been murdered by poison.

Boris had the means, as far as the medical knowledge was concerned, to choose which poison to use and how to administer it.

They still had to find a connection that put the poison into Boris's possession.

Boris had a motive to kill Chester in that his death allowed Boris to simply step into his position with a minimum of scrutiny.

They still needed to show that he not only had the opportunity to administer the poison, but when and how he had obtained it.

Once Boris was placed in Chester's job, he was in a position to carry out the theft of the security system. It would be no problem whatsoever for Boris to find a buyer for such a system who would be more than happy to pay any amount to gain such an advantage in the arms race and would gladly provide sanctuary to Boris with no questions asked.

When the team had last met, they had all come to the same conclusion. Whoever was supposed to have been on duty to receive the cargo in Afghanistan had to have been working with Boris. It made sense, but it was still speculation. The problem facing George was how to identify the person and prove the connection.

At this point, he didn't even have a name to go on. He knew he would have to be extremely careful not to raise any suspicion about what he was up to. Making a mistake in Afghanistan could cost him his life. George suspected that was the reason the senator had insisted on his contacting Omar Kadiere as soon as he arrived. He would know of ways to obtain information and would have the connections to make that happen.

George heard a bell sound and noticed that the *fasten seat belts* sign had been turned on. A moment later, an announcement came over the speaker that they were beginning their descent into the airport at Kabul. He put his notes in his briefcase and slid it under his seat. He raised and locked his tray table and fastened his seat belt. The flight crew walked throughout the plane assisting passengers as needed in preparation for landing. When that was done, they took their seats and fastened their seat belts. Air traffic was light; the pilot had to circle the field only once before he received the all clear to land.

As he left the plane, George thanked the crew for an excellent flight. He headed straight for baggage claim. The Kingman plant was located near Kandahar. George had been told a shuttle service would take him to his hotel just outside Kandahar. As it turned out, there were only two other passengers who were taking the shuttle with him.

CHAPTER 27

Trevor had all his notes spread out on the desk in front of him. His tie was loosened and his top shirt button was undone. His shirt sleeves were rolled up to his elbows and it was clear that he had run his hand through his tousled hair a number of times. He'd had a strange feeling all morning that there was something he had overlooked when he was in Philadelphia, and he couldn't shake the feeling. He had read all his notes at least twice and had intensely studied Boris's personnel file that Philip Croft had given him. Something was bugging him like a gnat that keeps buzzing around your head, staying just out of reach. He called Jordan's number.

"Jordan? This is Trevor. Have I caught you at a bad time?"

"No, this is actually a good time. I was about to take a break. Do you need something?"

"Yes. I can be there in about five minutes. Would you mind taking your break with me? I know there's something that I missed in Philadelphia, but I can't put my finger on it. It's driving me nuts. I feel like it's right in front of me, but I just can't see it."

"Sure. Come on over. I'll meet you in the cafeteria."

When Trevor arrived, Jordan was at a table with a cup of coffee. She looked relaxed in her dark-blue, calf-length skirt and blue-striped blouse. Since she had no meetings that day, she was wearing low-heeled sandals.

Trevor had rolled the sleeves of his shirt back down and straightened his tie and he had even put on his suit coat, but he still had that look of frustration on his face; the look that Jordan had seen before in her own mirror when she felt like the answer she was searching for was just out of reach.. He took his notes and the Philadelphia file on Boris out of his briefcase.

"Let's start at the beginning," Jordan said. "What were you going to Philadelphia to achieve?"

"To meet with Philip Croft, the warehouse manager, to find out what kind of employee Boris was," said Trevor. "Did he get along well with coworkers and supervisors? How much and what kind of training had he received. Did he work hard or was he a slacker? Basic questions like that. I also wanted to see Philip's reaction when I told him that Boris was being considered for a management position that required security clearance and I wanted to know what reasons Boris gave for requesting the transfer to the Arlington plant and why he had made the request at that particular time."

"And did you receive the answers to those questions?" asked Jordan.

"Yes I did, but I still keep feeling that there was something else I should have asked."

"You mentioned at a previous meeting that you wanted to know why Boris was hired in Philadelphia given the fact that he had quit his job at Higby," said Jordan.

"That's it!" said Trevor. "The file that Philip gave me doesn't mention Higby at all, and neither did Philip. I'm not sure that they even knew Boris had ever been employed at Higby. The file just shows that he came to Kingman to apply for a job. I'll call

Philip and raise that question with him. Thank you, Jordan. I don't know how I missed that, but now I can complete this part of the file."

"You're welcome," said Jordan. "It'll be interesting to see what you find out. If Philip tells you that they have no previous employment listed for Boris, will you tell him about Boris's employment at Higby?"

"No, I don't think so. If Boris lied to get that job, I don't think that should be discussed with anyone other than the three of us as this point. Since he's no longer in Philadelphia, no harm can come from their not knowing. I'll let you know what I find out," said Trevor.

When he returned to his office, he immediately placed a call to Philip Croft.

"Hello, Philip. I'm sorry to bother you again after having just left, but there was one question I forgot to ask."

"No problem. What do you need to know?"

"Had Boris mentioned any previous employment when he applied for a job with you? I can't find anything in the file about any previous employment, and that question was left blank on his application form."

"That shouldn't be," said Philip. "I can't understand why someone didn't catch that. Let me check on that and call you back this afternoon or first thing tomorrow, okay?"

"Fine. Thanks. I'm sure there must be a logical explanation as to what he'd previously done and why it hadn't been noted in his file. I'll be waiting to hear from you."

The next morning, Trevor got the call from Philip. "Hello, Philip. Did you find out why there was no record of Boris's previous employment in the file?"

"I've been through all our records on Boris three times. There's nothing that mentions any previous employment. I am at a loss to explain it. The only explanation I can offer is that the girl who took his application said that she just assumed it was his first job. I found out that she'd been recently hired herself after having just graduated from business school. It was her first job. To her, nothing about his application raised any questions. Needless to say, I explained to her that even if this is a person's first job, the application should state that in writing."

"Was it common knowledge she was a new employee?"

"Yes," said Philip. "She replaced a woman who had been in that position for about ten years. The woman's husband is in the military and had just received orders that he was being transferred to California. Will this have an effect on your investigation?"

"Not sure," said Trevor, "but thanks for your assistance, and please don't discuss this with anyone. I have more work to do, but I'll be in touch with you."

Trevor added this additional information to the notes that he had made from his trip to Philadelphia. He noted that it would have been very easy for Boris to have learned of the addition of the new clerk in personnel since the previous one was being given a large farewell party. By omitting any reference to his employment at Higby, Boris gave the appearance of a bright young man who would be an asset if hired. Trevor felt more than a little guilty about not sharing the information about Boris's previous employment with Philip, but he agreed with Jordan that they had to be careful about letting out information they had gathered until the case was complete. There was too much at stake, and since Boris was no longer working at the Philadelphia plant, there would be no harm done by not giving them all the facts then.

CHAPTER 28

I t was already night when George arrived at his hotel. He knew that he was tired, but his senses were running at full speed. He went over everything that he had to do, realizing how important it was that he not make any mistakes. He called room service and ordered a sandwich and a bottle of beer. He wasn't all that hungry, but he felt that eating something would help him to settle down so he would be able to sleep.

He planned to establish contact with the American embassy in the morning and then meet with Stanley Fremont. He'd left a seven thirty wake-up call with the front desk. Being in a different time zone, he didn't trust his inner clock to wake him at the appropriate time. While he waited for his snack to arrive, he turned on the television and found a sitcom that looked interesting. He didn't have long to wait until there was a knock on his door and a bellman announced that his food had arrived.

As he finished the last of his beer, he realized that the long hours of his day were finally catching up with him, so he took a hot shower and turned in for the night.

The sound of the phone ringing brought George out of a deep sleep the following morning. He got up and dressed and decided to place a call to Omar Kadiere at the American embassy before breakfast. He had been told that Omar was usually at work by seven o'clock. His room had a small electric pot for heating water along with packets of both coffee and tea. He fixed a cup of coffee and dialed Omar on his cell phone.

"Hello, this is Omar Kadiere."

"Hello. This is George Kilburn, Mr. Kadiere. I arrived from Virginia last night. Senator Granger suggested that I contact you before I head over to the Kingman Corporation to get started."

"Yes, the senator told me that you'd be calling this morning. Please call me Omar. Senator Granger gave me an overview of your mission here, and I assured him that I would make myself available for any assistance you might require."

"Thank you, Omar, and please call me George. At this point, I'm not sure what I may or may not require. I haven't been to the Kingman plant or spoken with any of our people yet."

"If I may make a suggestion," said Omar, "when you make contact with your people, tell them that you will be in contact with the American embassy here. You can say that a close friend has a son serving in the military here and you promised that you would try to contact him through the embassy. That is something that's done on a regular basis and will not give anyone cause to think anything unusual about it. It will also provide a reason for multiple contacts if need be."

"Thanks. I'll do that. I think that I should have a fair idea of where I stand and what I need to do after I meet with Stanley Fremont and have a chance to look over their shipping documents. I must admit that I feel better just having established contact with the embassy."

"I understand completely," said Omar. "Knowing that you are not on home soil and are unable to understand everything that people say to you can be very disconcerting."

"I agree. I'll probably contact you either this afternoon or this evening. I believe Senator Granger mentioned that he had given you my cell phone number. I'm using only that phone to contact you. It will always be with me."

"Yes, he did give me the number, and I think that it's wise to limit our conversations to that phone," said Omar. "It will be much more difficult to trace. I will be waiting to hear from you. Have a good day."

"Thanks, and the same to you."

George used his room phone to place a call to the Kingman plant and request that the shuttle be sent to transport him to the plant. He figured he would have enough time for breakfast before a car arrived.

The Kingman plant was located about ten miles north and east of Kandahar. The shuttle dropped him off at the entrance to the main warehouse where he was to meet with Stanley Fremont, the warehouse manager. Mr. Fremont was on the phone when George was shown into his office, so George took a seat at the table where it appeared Stanley did most of his work. There were stacks of folders sitting at one end and maps of the region on the wall behind the table.

As he hung up the phone, Stanley stood and walked over to the table with his hand extended. He was a rugged- looking man just under six feet tall with dark-brown hair.

"Good morning," he said. "You must be George Kilburn. I'm Stanley Fremont. Welcome to Afghanistan. I trust that your hotel accommodations are satisfactory."

"Good morning, Stanley," said George. "Yes, the hotel is very nice, thanks. I need to know if this room is secure for our discussions."

"Yes, it's secure. I personally checked everything out myself. From time to time, we come in contact with highly classified documents or materials, so we have designated areas for dealing with such things. This office is one such area, so you needn't be concerned about anything that's said in here."

"Good to know," said George. "If you need to contact me when I'm away from here, be sure to use my cell phone rather than leaving a message with the hotel. I believe you have the number. I understand you've been briefed as to the true nature of my visit as well as the reason that'll be given to everyone else."

"Yes, I've spoken at length with Tom Clancy. I understand the need for secrecy and will do whatever I can to assist you. Have you been in touch with the embassy yet?"

"Yes. I spoke with Omar before coming here this morning," said George. "I'd appreciate it if the information about my staying for a few days for personal reasons to meet with the embassy could be leaked to the grapevine right away."

"Consider it done," said Stanley. "Now, what do you need to know?"

"Who was on duty and actually received the cargo?"

"His name is Rashi Mubarek. He's been in the shipping department for about two years. He's a good worker and gets along with his coworkers. He was called in at the last minute because the regular employee had been in an automobile accident the night before. He's still in the hospital with a broken leg and a number of bruises. He's expected to make a full recovery, but we don't know how long he will be out.

"I was on duty when the shipment came in. Rashi went through the correct steps to check the arriving shipment. He pulled the shipping manifest and compared the items listed with the items received. That was when he found that there were items received that weren't listed. He went online and pulled up the requisition forms. They all listed just the items that appeared on the manifest. He followed all of the required steps to determine that this wasn't just a filing mix-up or an honest shipping mistake. When he found nothing to explain the additional cargo, he immediately reported it to me to receive instructions about how to handle it. I instructed him to have the cargo moved to a designated secured location and to continue with his other duties. I told him I'd take over from there on. I went to the location and opened the shipping containers. It was at that point that I saw that the containers held the security system, operating manuals, and hardware.

"I've had all of the paperwork we have on file pulled for you to go through, and I've put you in a secure office with a desk and a copy machine. I haven't assigned a clerk to help you since I've been instructed to treat this as a top-priority case with minimum exposure. I can, however, provide someone if you wish."

"No, but thank you. I can make any copies I need, and we need to keep this known by as few people as possible," said George. "Who's the employee that Rashi replaced?"

"His name is Josef Danforth. He's been working in the shipping department for the past six years. He works well with the other employees and is always ready to lend a helping hand whenever needed. He's well liked and shows good promise as a future manager. The personnel folders on both of these employees are included with the other paperwork waiting for you in your office."

"Thank you," said George. "It looks like you've given me plenty to get started on. The only thing left for me to do is to stop talking and get to work."

"I had the phone set up so that you can reach me by just pressing the intercom button," said Stanley. "You can call outside by dialing nine, but that line isn't secure."

Stanley led the way to an office just down the hall. George noticed that there was a clean coffee mug sitting on the desk.

"There's a break room just across the hall where we have a twenty-four hour coffee machine," Stanley said as he turned and headed back to his office.

CHAPTER 29

George removed the most-recent requisitions from the stack of documents that he had been given, noting the dates of submission, the person making the request, and listing the items that had been requested.

Next, he removed the freight manifests, which showed the items requested and whether they were in stock and had been shipped or whether they would need to be ordered from another warehouse.

As George suspected, the requisition and the shipping manifest that covered the shipment in question did not list the erroneously shipped items. He made a note to ask Stanley if Rashi worked at his own desk when he took over Josef's duties or if he moved to Josef's desk to handle those duties. Based on the way Boris had switched documents when he was working at Higby International Freight Company, and hidden them in his locker, George wasn't ruling out the possibility of the same thing happening in Afghanistan. He made a mental note of where he would look.

The next items he reviewed were the personnel files for Rashi and Josef. He made notes on each file covering their ages, where they had been born, if and where each man had attended college, their previous employment, and whether either of them had any previous encounters with the law. He made a note to call Jordan and have Sasha do a genealogical search on Josef; he wanted to know if there was any connection between Josef and Boris.

He was busy studying the documents and didn't notice Stanley standing in the doorway. "Knock, knock," said Stanley. "Are you interested in getting some lunch?"

George looked at his watch and was surprised to find that it was midafternoon. "Yes. This is actually a good time for a break. Lunch sounds good."

"We have a good cafeteria here," said Stanley, "but if you want to talk, I suggest a restaurant down the street that I enjoy. Both the food and the service are good and the price is cheap."

"It sounds like my kind of place," said George. "Does this office lock? I have a lot of papers spread out that I'd rather nobody looked at."

"Yes," said Stanley. "I have the key in my desk. Be right back."

Stanley returned shortly with the key. George locked the office and they left for lunch.

While they were walking, Stanley asked if George had gotten everything he needed.

"It looks like it," said George. "I wanted to ask you if Rashi works at his own desk when he's working on Josef's duties or does he move to Josef's desk."

"He works at his own desk. There's no reason for him to change desks. When the requisitions, freight manifests, or bills of lading come in, everything's together in one package. All he needs is a pen to initial each section as he completes his verification and a calculator to double check the amounts charged and he has his own. All the employees do."

"I'd like to go through Josef's desk after everyone leaves tonight," said George, "if that's all right with you."

"Sure. No problem. May I ask what you're looking for?"

"I'm not entirely sure myself," said George. "It may be nothing, but I have a hunch, and I'd like to check it out."

"I'll let you know when everyone's left for the day," said Stanley. "I'll wait in my office while you do what you need to. If anybody comes by, I'll keep them busy."

"Thanks. I appreciate that."

It was about six thirty when the phone rang on George's desk. "All clear," said Stanley. "The last person just left."

George walked down the hall to the accounting office where both Rashi and Josef worked. Every employee had their own cubical that contained a desk, a filing cabinet, a trash basket, a three-shelf bookcase, and two chairs. On each desk sat a telephone, a desk light, and a calculator. The employees were allowed to personalize their cubicles with family pictures, calendars, and plants.

George began his search by going through each drawer of the desk looking at and under everything. As he opened each drawer, he not only looked at the contents inside, but he also checked to see if anything was taped to the bottom of the drawer. Next, he checked the bookcase, being just as methodical as he was with the desk. Finally, he went through the file cabinet. He had completed two of the four drawers and was examining the third drawer. Something didn't feel right. The drawer didn't appear to be as deep as the other drawers. When he removed the contents, there were fewer items than he removed from the first two drawers.

As he felt around inside the drawer, he discovered that this drawer had a false bottom in it. It took him a few minutes to figure out how to remove the bottom, but when he did, he knew that his hunch had paid off. He removed a sealed folder from the drawer.

Inside the folder were duplicate copies of the requisition, the freight manifest and the bill of lading for the shipment in question except that these documents also contained the erroneously shipped items.

Now that he had proof that this had not been a shipping mistake, but a well thought out plan to steal a top military security system, he knew that he had to act quickly.

CHAPTER 30

George took out his cell phone and dialed Stanley's number.

"Hello. Fremont here," said the voice on the other end of the line.

"Stanley, this is George. I need you to come to Josef's cubicle right away."

"I'll be right there."

When Stanley arrived, George showed him what he had discovered. Needless to say, Stanley was dumfounded.

"How'd you know?"

George explained how Boris had been previously employed at Higby International and had pulled this same scheme there.

"Do you have a connection between Josef and Boris?" asked Stanley.

"Not yet," said George. "That's the next step. It's imperative that you don't discuss this with anyone."

"Yes of course. Just tell me what you want me to do."

"Thank you," said George. "The only thing I need right now is for you to keep tabs on when Josef is getting out of the hospital. I'm going to see if I can get him an extended stay. I want to keep the originals of these documents and if Josef gets out of the hospital and returns to work, he could easily find out that they are missing from his hiding place. I can't have that happen."

George put the documents in his briefcase and put the false bottom back in the drawer. He restored everything else to the way he had found it. He and Stanley returned to George's office. George thanked Stanley for his cooperation, and Stanley headed home. George had a couple of calls to make before he would be ready to leave.

George called Omar on his private line at the embassy from his cell phone.

"Hello, Kadiere speaking."

"Omar, this is George Kilburn. We need to talk."

"Take a cab to the M. Basse Restaurant," said Omar. "Give the maître d' your name, and say you'd like a table in the dining room. I'll meet you there. If you like, we can even order dinner. The food is very good."

"Thanks," said George. "I have one call to make before I leave. See you shortly."

George dialed Jordan's number at the office and hoped she was there to take the call. He knew that it was mid-morning and there was a chance that she might be away from her desk. He needed to talk to her about the case, and he also just wanted to hear her voice.

It was midmorning. Jordan was in her office going over the latest information she'd received from Trevor. He told her that he had learned from Philip Croft in Philadelphia that they never knew Boris had been previously employed before he started working there. Jordan was adding this information to her notes and was preparing an updated outline of events when the phone rang.

"Hello", she said.

"Hello, Jordan. This is George. How are you?"

"George, it's good to hear from you! How's your trip going? Did you have a good flight? What time is it there?"

"Slow down," he said, laughing. "It's good to hear your voice. The trip over was long but good. It's seven thirty here, and I'm meeting Omar Kadiere for dinner after we finish talking. If my calculations are correct, it should be about eleven thirty in the morning there."

"Your calculations are perfect," she said. "Your timing is good as well. I was just preparing an updated outline of events to share with you when you called. Trevor has obtained some interesting information."

Jordan told George about her meeting with Trevor and his follow-up conversation with Philip Croft. "Trevor confirmed that it was common knowledge that the person who took and processed Boris's application was new to the job, so his neglecting to mention his previous employment slipped right by her." She also let George know that Trevor had decided not to let Philadelphia know about Boris's previous employment at this time. Since Boris no longer worked there, it would accomplish nothing, and they could be informed later.

"You're right, that is very interesting information," said George. "I have some news too. I've been through all of the paperwork here, from the initial requisitions to the freight manifest forms and the bills of lading. Everything looked to be on the up and up until I went through Josef Danforth's cubicle after everyone left for the night."

"Who is Josef Danforth?"

"Josef is the person who was supposed to have received the shipment. It was only because he was in the hospital due to an automobile accident that someone new was handling his duties. While I was going through the filing cabinet, I found that one of the drawers had a false bottom. I removed the bottom and found another set of documents consisting of the requisition, freight manifest, and bill of lading for the shipment in question; only this set included the missing cargo. Josef did exactly the same thing Boris had done at Higby International. Josef is still in the hospital from his accident, and I'm going to see if Omar has any suggestions as to how we can prolong his stay. While he's in the hospital, I can work without having to put the documents back in the filing cabinet."

"That's great work," said Jordan. "Is there anything we can do here to help?"

"Have you been able to check the telephone logs after Boris's promotion to disbursement officer to see if he made or received any international calls?

"Yes, and there were no calls. Also, Kingman does not obtain cell phone numbers unless the person's job requires that they be available twenty four hours a day and the disbursement officer's job is not one of those jobs. Shaun believes that even if they had a cell phone number for Boris, it is unlikely that he would use it to make those calls. Boris would most likely use a burn phone."

"I think he right about that, but thanks for checking. I also want you to have Sasha run a genealogical search on Josef Danforth. We need to find a connection between him and Boris. I want to know if he has ties of any kind to India, friends, relatives or even as a favorite vacation spot."

"I'll put her on that right away," said Jordan. "Do you have any idea how much longer you'll be there?"

"No I don't. It'll depend on how things go from here. Bring Trevor up to date, but for now, let's keep this information between the three of us. We can't afford any leaks, no matter how small or unintentional. If Sasha asks about why you're looking at Josef, let her think it's routine."

"If she's told he's an employee at that plant, she won't ask further. She knows that we're checking everyone out just to be thorough," said Jordan.

"Good. I'm hanging up. Omar might begin to wonder if he's been stood up. When Sasha finishes running the genealogical search on Josef, hold it until I contact you. I want to get a secure line at the embassy to have that sent to. I'll call you back in a couple of days. In the meanwhile, just know that I'm thinking of you."

"I miss you, too" said Jordan. "Please be safe. I'll talk with you soon."

Jordan walked out of her office to see if Sasha was interested in going to lunch. When she looked at her watch, she realized that she had been on the phone with George for almost an hour, and she knew Sasha would have already left. She decided to go to the cafeteria for soup and a salad. When she came back, she would put Sasha on her new genealogical search. She would also call Trevor to bring him up to date on what George had told her.

Before heading up to the cafeteria, Jordan paused to add this most recent information from George to her notes. With things happening as quickly as they seemed to be, she didn't want to take any chance of forgetting anything. She left a message for Sasha rather than waiting until she returned from lunch to have her begin a new genealogical search. It would look more like a routine assignment that way, Jordan figured.

The information George had uncovered proved there was no longer any question about the cargo being sent to Afghanistan by accident. This was a well thought out plan to steal highly classified government property that could result in the loss of countless lives and millions of dollars.

Jordan realized she was more than a little concerned about George's safety. The stakes were climbing higher. Anyone who could accomplish something like the cargo diversion would have no problem killing anyone who got in his way or tried to stop him. Jordan shuddered at the thought that at least one murder had been committed. Leaving the new assignment on Sasha's desk, Jordan headed for the cafeteria.

CHAPTER 31

When Sasha returned from lunch, she found the note from Jordan about doing a genealogical search on Josef Danforth. She didn't have any more than the name to go by, but she received three hits when she put his name in. How to determine if any of these were the person she was looking for was the challenge she was facing.

The first Josef Danforth was a seventy-five-year-old man who had been born in Florida, graduated from Florida State University with a degree in psychology, was married with four grown sons and daughters, and had retired after twenty-five years as a social worker with the State of Florida. Nothing indicated he had any knowledge of or connections with the type of work or activities she had found with Boris Urich.

The second man spelled his first name with a *ph* at the end rather than an *f*. He had died five years earlier in a traffic accident in Chicago.

The remaining Josef Danforth was a man who was approximately the same age as Boris. This one had been born in India and had come to the United States to study medicine. He had attended Med Start Junior College in Maryland before pursuing a medical degree at Johns Hopkins. The records also showed that, at one time, Josef had worked for Higby International Freight Company. He had an uncle who was employed in a midlevel position at the Indian embassy in Kabul, and Josef had lived with him for several years. Sasha remembered that Boris had attended Med Start and was previously employed at Higby International. Was it a coincidence that Josef and Boris had attended the same school and been employed by the same company? Sasha knew that Jordan didn't believe in coincidence. She knew that she had come across something Jordan would want to know immediately. She was considering calling Jordan when Jordan came through the door.

"Hi," said Sasha. "I've found something you'll be interested in." Sasha handed Jordan the information she had just printed out. "This appears to be the Josef Danforth you're looking for."

`"You're kidding!" said Jordan as she skimmed the printout. "I need to check this against what we have on Boris to see if their school and work ties occurred at the same time and if there are any other connections. Good work, Sasha! See if you can find a website for Med Start Junior College in Maryland. Sometimes, smaller schools publish their yearbooks and class pictures online either as a group or individually. I'd like to find out if these guys are photogenic. While you're doing that, I'm going to give Andrew Jorgensen another call and see if the good professor remembers Josef Danforth."

Jordan went through her notes for Jorgensen's phone number and dialed it.

The phone was ringing for the third time when a man answered.

"Hello, this is Professor Jorgensen."

"Hello, Professor Jorgensen, this is Jordan Anderson. I don't know if you remember me, but we spoke a few weeks back about one of your former students, Boris Urich."

"Yes, I remember you," said the professor. "As I recall, you were doing a background check because Boris was under consideration for a high-security job. Is there a problem with his clearance?"

"This call isn't actually about Boris," said Jordan. "I was wondering if you remember another young man who attended school there, possibly at the same time as Boris. His name is Josef Danforth. They may have been friends."

"Yes, I remember Mr. Danforth," said professor Jorgensen. "He was a bright student. He and Boris were always together. I assumed it was because of their mutual interests, and of course they were both studying to become doctors. After Boris dropped out of medical school, Mr. Danforth continued and eventually graduated from Johns Hopkins."

"Did they have mutual interests other than attending medical school?" asked Jordan.

"Yes, now that I think about it, I always felt that it was odd that Mr. Danforth was so captivated with rare and fatal diseases, just as Boris was."

"Why did that strike you as odd?" asked Jordan. "Isn't that just another part of studying medicine?"

"Well, yes it is," said the professor. "It's just that Mr. Danforth was studying to become a general practitioner and had never said anything about going into research. It seemed highly unlikely that he would ever come across rare and toxic diseases in a family practice. Then again, he wasn't from this country, and maybe he thought that knowledge would be useful to him."

Jordan had been taking notes as fast as she could write when, suddenly, she ran out of ink. She quickly took another pen from a wire container sitting on her desk and continued taking notes.

"I remember that the two of them would spend hours trying to outdo each other in finding the most unusual and lethal diseases that a person could contract. I once teased them that they should consider a secondary field of study as mystery writers since they'd found so many ways a person could be killed. We had a good laugh at that. Like I said, Josef went on to graduate from Johns Hopkins and Boris dropped out of medical school. I lost track of them after that."

"Thank you so much for speaking with me," said Jordan. "It's been a pleasure talking with you."

"I hope I was helpful," said the professor. "Sometimes, I start talking and just ramble on. It was nice speaking with you again, Jordan. Feel free to call any time. Good bye."

"You were very helpful, professor. Thank you and good bye."

While Jordan had been on the phone with Professor Jorgensen, Sasha had been looking up Med Start Junior College on the Internet. Its website had obviously been designed to attract students to the school. Photos showed modern buildings nestled in a beautifully landscaped campus a few miles outside Towson, Maryland. It wasn't a very large school, but it offered a curriculum slanted toward preparing students for going on to study medicine at Johns Hopkins University, a strong incentive for serious students with visions of stethoscopes dancing in their heads.

Each year, the graduating class had a group portrait taken that showed the students dressed in white lab coats. She saw a photo of the most recent graduates and was able to navigate to photos of earlier graduates by year. Sasha found the photo of Josef's graduating class. She clicked on a button to enlarge the picture and printed it out. When Sasha saw Jordan was off the phone, she took the printout to her and pointed to one particular graduate.

"This is Boris?" Jordan asked.

"Yes."

"Good work, Sasha."

"There's a machine on the second floor that can extract and enlarge a portion of a picture. It should be able to do that with this picture and give us a larger picture of just Josef. I can't run the machine, but I know someone who can. I'm sure that it will be no problem getting him to single out Josef's picture if you want me to."

"Yes, that would be helpful, Sasha. Thank you," said Jordan.

Jordan knew George would want to follow up with Omar about Josef's uncle having held a midlevel position at the Indian embassy, and the picture of Josef might be helpful. Most important, they had established a connection between Boris and Josef.

Jordan wanted to bring Trevor up to date with their findings as George had asked her to do. She placed a call to his office but his secretary had said that he was in a meeting. Jordan left her cell number and asked the secretary to tell Trevor to call back anytime, even after hours.

Sasha returned in an hour with the enlarged picture of Josef. "I had to wait for a few minutes for my friend to finish another job before he was able to start on this," she said as she handed the picture to Jordan.

"He did a great job," said Jordan. "Please thank him. I'm sure this will be useful to George. He'll call when he's able to get a secure line. I can send our updated information to him then. "I was wondering," said Jordan. "What reason did you give your friend about why you wanted this person's picture removed from the group and enlarged? Wasn't he curious?"

"Yes he was," said Sasha, smiling. "I said that a friend of mine had been contacted for a blind date with him," said Sasha, "and she wanted to know what he looked like before she agreed to meet him."

"Good answer," said Jordan. "I think I'll call it a day. I have some things I need to pick up on the way home and I would like to avoid the traffic".

Jordan loaded her briefcase. She was happy they had established a link between Boris and Josef and wondered where that would lead. Was the information Sasha found about Josef's uncle working at the Indian embassy going to lead them to any snake venom? If so, would that put George in danger? Stopping only to say good night to Sasha, she headed out the door for home with those questions in mind.

CHAPTER 32

George picked up his cell phone and called the embassy. "Hello, Omar. I'm leaving the office and should arrive at the restaurant in about twenty minutes."

"Fine," said Omar. "I may be a little longer than that. Get a table in the bar area. I'll find you when I arrive. I shouldn't be more than thirty minutes behind you."

"Will do," said George.

When he arrived at the restaurant, George left his name with the maître d' and said that he was expecting Omar Kadiere to be meeting him shortly. The maître d' knew Mr. Kadiere and assured George that he would show him to the table as soon as he arrived.

When Omar arrived, George was sipping a scotch on the rocks and munching on peanuts from the bowl that had been brought to the table with his drink. After he had greeted George and ordered a martini, Omar sat down and loosened his tie.

"So," began Omar, "have you been successful in getting the information you need?"

"Things are going well so far. Stanley Fremont has been most helpful. My problem is that for every answer I find, I come up with another question."

"Is there anything that I can help you with?" asked Omar.

"Yes, actually, there is. Josef's time in the hospital has been a blessing in disguise. The fact that someone else had to take over receipt of the shipment containing the unscheduled cargo is the only reason we found out about the theft in the first place. It appears that Josef's replacement, Rashi, wasn't involved and knew nothing about the unlisted cargo."

"Are you sure that Josef knew about and was involved in the shipping of the unlisted cargo?" asked Omar.

"I am now. I asked Stanley and learned that when Rashi was handling Josef's workload, he had everything he needed at his own desk and therefore had no reason to work at Josef's.

When the paperwork came through, it was simply placed in Rashi's in-box rather than Josef's. There's a cover sheet with all the paperwork listing the name of the person responsible for processing that shipment. That's for mail distribution purposes. While Josef's name was shown as the responsible party, Rashi signed under Josef's name to show that he actually handled it that day. Once I learned that, I arranged with Stanley to let me know when everyone had left for the day."

George explained how he had searched and found a drawer in Josef's file cabinet with a false bottom in it. The altered paperwork was hidden inside. "I then called Stanley to come to Josef's desk and witness what I had discovered. I have these documents in my possession and this brings me to the first favor I need from you.

I understand that Josef's injuries are on the mend and he will be released, possibly as soon as tomorrow. I need him to stay in the hospital for now so that I can hold onto the evidence that I removed from his workspace. I want to keep possession of the originals, and I don't want Josef to find out that I have them. Is that something you could help with?"

"Yes," said Omar. "As it turns out, one person in the other car died from the accident. I can put the word out that it's suspected that the deceased had a highly contagious disease. That should keep Josef quarantined for at least a week, maybe two. What else?"

"I need a secure line to have some documents sent to me," said George. "Can you give me one at the embassy?"

"Done," said Omar. "You can have your documents sent to my private line. If you want, we can go to the embassy after dinner if the documents are ready to be sent."

"My associate has probably left the office for the day," said George. "I think tomorrow would be better if that works with your schedule."

"Tomorrow it is," said Omar. "I'll give you the number now in case you speak to your associate later tonight. The documents can be sent any time. No one sees what comes in on that line but myself, and I'll call you on your cell phone as soon as they arrive."

When they finished dinner, George insisted on picking up the check. Omar gave George one of his cards, making sure that he added his private number. They agreed to meet at the embassy at four o'clock the following afternoon. They left the restaurant and said good night.

CHAPTER 33

The next morning, Jordan was at the office bright and early. She wanted to get everything that she was sending to George in the proper order and to make sure that she hadn't overlooked any details. Considering the time difference, Jordan figured that he'd probably call her about nine o'clock. It would be close to the end of the day for him, so she wanted to have everything ready to be faxed as soon as she had the phone number.

It was about eight forty-five when his call came to her cell phone. One look at the screen on her phone and she knew that it was George.

"Good morning George," she said. "We're having a beautiful, sunny day here. It's about fifty-eight degrees outside right now and will be up to sixty-nine degrees by late afternoon."

"Good morning yourself," said George. "It's raining and about forty-five degrees here. If you're ready, I have the fax number for the documents."

"I'm ready."

George gave her the number that he had been given by Omar. Jordan hung up the phone and proceeded to fax the documents. Finally, the last page completed the cycle; and she received a coded sheet telling her that the pages had been received. A few minutes later, George called to let her know that he'd received the documents.

"Did everything come through all right?" she asked.

"Yes," said George. "I'm looking at them as we speak."

"As you'll see, Sasha's Internet search for Josef Danforth proved to be fruitful. I was surprised to find that Josef had also worked for Higby International Freight Company. You'll see that Josef has an uncle employed in a mid level position with the Indian embassy in Kabul and Josef lived with him for several years. I hope Omar can shed some light on that."

"That may prove to be the missing link to India and the snake venom," said George.

"The photo of Danforth was taken when he graduated from Med Start. I'm not sure if that helps, but I sent it anyway."

"The information you and Sasha have provided will be very helpful. Thank Sasha for me, and tell her I'm taking the two of you to a nice restaurant for lunch when I return."

"We'll hold you to that," said Jordan. "Oh, by the way, I tried to call Trevor, but he was in a meeting and hasn't called me back yet."

"I'm sure he will as soon as he can."

"Keep in touch and let me know if you need anything else from here," said Jordan. "Bye for now."

While George was obtaining the documents from Jordan, Omar had stepped out of the room to allow him to talk privately. When the last of the documents had come in and George had completed the call, Omar came back into the room.

"I take it that everything came through successfully," he said.

"Yes it did," said George. "I'm grateful for your assistance. There's one last thing I have to ask of you. Part of the information that came through concerns an online search that was done on

Josef Danforth. It shows that he has an uncle who is employed in a mid-level position with the Indian embassy in Kabul. Josef lived with him for several years. Being an embassy employee, his information isn't available to us with an ordinary computer search. I'd appreciate it if you could see what you can find concerning the uncle. His last name is also Danforth, but I don't have a first name. I need as much as you can find concerning where and when he lived in India, when and how he came to be with the Indian embassy, what he did for a living prior to coming to the embassy, and anything you can find concerning his family."

"I'm sure I can help you there," said Omar. "I'll put my secretary on that first thing tomorrow. She's very trustworthy, so you needn't be concerned about the inquiry being discovered."

Having successfully faxed all the information she and Sasha had gathered to George, Jordan incorporated this information into the other information they had obtained. Her concentration was broken by the sound of her phone ringing.

"Hi Jordan, this is Trevor. I'm sorry that I missed you yesterday. Have you heard from George? How's the case progressing?"

"Hi Trevor. I just spoke with George a few minutes ago, and the case is going very well so far, but I think he'll be happy when he can return home. I was calling you yesterday to bring you up to date on what we've learned so far. Would you have some free time today?"

"Yes," said Trevor. "I can pick you up in front of your building at twelve thirty. We can talk over lunch. I know of a place just south of here where they have soup and salad."

"I know that place. George and I have eaten there and you're right, the food is good. I'll see you out front at twelve thirty."

At twelve twenty, Jordan stopped at Sasha's desk to let her know she was meeting with Trevor for lunch and could be reached on her cell phone if anything came up. She had just walked out the front door when Trevor pulled over to the curb and leaned over to open the door for her.

"Hi," he said, smiling. "Going my way?"

"You bet," she said as she got in. "How's your day been?"

"Good," said Trevor. "It's good to see you again."

The traffic was light. They got to the restaurant quickly and were seated right away. They placed their orders, and Jordan began to bring Trevor up to speed concerning the case.

As she progressed from the material Sasha had found on Josef Danforth, her own follow-up discussion with Professor Jorgensen at Med Start, and the fake duplicate copies of documents that George had discovered in the hidden section of a drawer in Josef's file cabinet, she showed Trevor the documents or copies of documents that substantiated their findings. She finished by telling Trevor what George had asked Omar to assist him with.

"I'm impressed," said Trevor. "This case is really coming together. Have you laid out things we still need to obtain?"

"Not yet. That's what I was about to do when you called. We can do that now if you'd like."

"Sure," said Trevor. "First, let me get the waitress to bring us some coffee." As soon as the coffee had been served, Jordan had her notebook ready to begin writing.

"I'll start off," said Trevor.

"We know that Chester didn't die of natural causes. He was murdered.

We know that Chester was poisoned using a rare snake venom.

We don't know how the venom was obtained or by whom. Hopefully, when we obtain more information about Josef's uncle, we can find the answer to that question. We suspect that Boris put poisonous snake venom on a needle or dart that was used to puncture Chester's neck.

We know that Josef and Boris both have medical backgrounds and a workable knowledge of poisons and lethal diseases that kill."

"I think we have enough proof that Boris, with the help of Josef, stole the security-system cargo and altered requisitions and shipping documents for the purpose of sending the cargo to Afghanistan to be sold for money and/or power," said Jordan.

"We know that Josef lived with his uncle in India for several years and that India is the only place where the snake that produces the venom discovered in Chester Rafferty's blood can be found.

We know that, with Chester dead, Boris was automatically put into a position where he could and did manipulate the sending of top-secret security system cargo to Afghanistan where it could be sold," concluded Jordan.

"Finally," said Trevor, "we need to know whether Josef's uncle was involved in any of this. Hopefully, Omar will be able to assist George in determining this."

CHAPTER 34

Being true to his word, Omar had called a good friend who happened to be one of the directors of the hospital where Josef Danforth was a patient. Following their conversation, a quarantine sign suddenly appeared on the door to Josef's room. Josef was told that the person in the other car involved in the accident was thought to have had a highly contagious disease and that until he was thoroughly checked out, he could not be released from the hospital. He was told that this procedure should be completed in a week to ten days.

The U.S. embassy in Kabul maintained a listing of all embassies and their staffs. When Omar's secretary looked at the Indian embassy listing, she found the name of Lomar Danforth. He was listed as being in his mid-fifties and had been employed by the embassy for the past thirty years.

"Seeing this has reminded me of a friend who, I believe, may know Lomar," Omar told George. "I'll contact him and see if I can obtain some additional information."

"Thank you," said George. "I appreciate that."

While Omar went to contact his friend, George studied the documents that Jordan had faxed to him. A short while later, Omar returned.

"I was correct," said Omar. "My friend has known Lomar for many years and speaks very highly of him. When I explained why I was asking about Lomar, he said he would come here and speak with you in person."

About thirty minutes later, a man was shown into the room where they were sitting. He was about five feet, eight inches tall with jet-black hair and a neatly trimmed mustache. His skin was dark and rugged from years of working outdoors. He wore khaki trousers and a pale-green shirt.

George and Omar both stood when he entered the room. After shaking his hand, Omar turned to introduce him to George as Khan DaSilva.

"I appreciate your taking time to talk with me," said George.

"I have known Lomar Danforth since we were both very young men. "When Omar told me of your interest in him, I was happy to come and speak with you. We both came to the embassy as teenagers doing manual labor in exchange for food and a place to sleep. Our parents had been farmers, but the land was so poor that almost nothing would grow in it."

"Do you live close enough that you keep in touch on a regular basis?" asked George.

"Lomar stays pretty busy with his work, so we can't always spend time together" said Khan.

"What kind of work does Lomar do?"

"He works in an office that comes under the jurisdiction of the embassy of India. He is a hard worker. His job is to settle disputes between people and business when they can't agree. He has a reputation for being fair and for resolving disputes quickly."

"Does he have a wife and family?" asked George.

"Lomar never married, but he is legal guardian to a nephew, Josef. Lomar's brother and sister-in-law lived in a rural area some thirty miles or so outside of Orissa and near the Bay of Bengal. A plague swept through the region and nearly wiped out the entire village where Josef's family lived. Josef was spared, but both of his parents died. That was when he went to live with his uncle."

"What kind of plague was it that took Josef's parents?" asked George.

"Nobody knew much about the virus that killed his parents," Khan answered. "After they died, Josef became obsessed with finding out all he could about every type of poison or virus that he could identify. I assume that was what made him decide to study medicine.

"After he moved in with his uncle," Omar inserted, "a pamphlet came in the embassy mail about a six-week seminar that was to be given in San Francisco, California, USA, during the month of August. The seminar was being taught by Dr. Anwar Thorn and was titled: *Identify and discuss the ten least common, known causes of death of people living in primitive areas.*

"Dr. Thorn lived and conducted his research in a village that was not far from the one where Josef had lived with his parents. He had written numerous papers and had traveled all over the world giving lectures on a number of the studies he had conducted."

"That's right," said Khan. "The topic, alone, fascinated Josef, and he became obsessed with attending it. His uncle used his influence with the embassy to obtain a spot for Josef at the seminar and to obtain a grant to help cover expenses. After the seminar, Josef found out that Dr. Thorn would soon be returning to the village where he had conducted his studies. In the end, it was agreed that Josef would travel to the village and study under the guidance of Dr. Thorn. He worked there until he returned to the United States to attend medical school. Josef is still close with his uncle and sees him whenever he can."

"Thank you for coming to talk with me," said George to Khan. "You've been very helpful, and it's been a pleasure to meet you."

"I'm glad I could help," said Khan. "Tell Josef that I hope he gets well soon."

After Khan left, George continued talking with Omar, "Does Dr. Thorn still work in the area?" he asked.

"As a matter of fact, I found out that Dr. Thorn is now at the village and will be there for another three weeks before starting his next teaching tour. You can get to the village by jeep in about five hours. I can arrange for a jeep and a driver who speaks the language and knows the customs. I'll set it up for tomorrow morning."

The next morning, George called Stanley Fremont on his cell phone to let him know what he had found out and where he was going. He thought about calling Jordan, as well, but decided to wait until he returned. He had no way of knowing what he was walking into or how the people might react to a stranger asking questions, and he didn't want to give Jordan any reason to worry.

The jeep and driver were waiting outside his hotel when he came out at nine o'clock. They arrived at the village in just over five hours. The doctor worked in a mud house. These houses, as the name implies are made of mud. The people use local materials to build them, with no plumbing or proper sewer systems. The roof is flat and is built using wooden poles and then coated with a mixture of mud and straws. Since this was a medical facility as well as his home, the doctor had made certain adjustments to the standard structure. He had brought in locking, medal cabinets to hold his medical supplies and serums and he had fresh water brought in that was kept in special containers to keep it pure. When they reached the doctor's hut, the front door was standing open. George looked around as he entered and, at first, he thought no one was there.

"Hello?" he called out. "Is anyone here?"

"I'll be right with you" came a voice from the back of the hut..

George looked up as a man came in from a back room. He was dressed in faded tan slacks and a light-brown shirt with the sleeves rolled up just above his elbows. His hair was down just past his shoulders. Today, it was pulled back into a pony tail tied at the base of his neck.

"Hello! Can I help you?"

"I hope so," said George. "Are you Dr. Anwar Thorn?"

"Yes I am Dr. Thorn."

George identified himself and explained that he was making inquiries about a young man who had attended his seminar in San Francisco. "The young man's name is Josef Danforth."

"Yes, I remember that seminar," said Dr. Thorn, "and I remember Josef. When I returned after that seminar, he came here to study with me for several months. Later, he left to return to the United States to attend medical school. Why are you asking about him? Is he all right?"

"He was recently involved in an automobile accident," said George, "and is in the hospital. He's expected to make a complete recovery from his injuries. A person in the other car, however, was killed and is thought to have had a highly contagious disease. Josef's family used to live in a village near here, and since you're knowledgeable about the diseases in this area, I wanted to make sure we checked out every possibility. Anything that you can share with me could be helpful, even if it seems insignificant. Did you, by chance, have any handouts at the seminar that listed the diseases you covered?"

"Yes I did," said Dr. Thorn. "I'll give you a copy of our handout if you think it will help. It lists each disease, the cause, the symptoms, and the remedy if there is one."

"What reasons do you have for choosing the particular diseases you do?" George asked.

"Since these are diseases that are known to originate in this region, I feel these seminars are necessary. As I'm sure you know, just because a disease originates in one location doesn't mean that it can't be taken to another."

"That's an interesting point," said George.

"Most doctors aren't trained in diseases that might affect only a small percentage of their patient base," continued Dr. Thorn. "To me, that's just narrow thinking, so I do what I can." he said, as he handed George the pamphlet.

"Please give Josef my best wishes for a speedy recovery. He was one of my most interested students, always asking questions and making notes; like he couldn't learn fast enough. I had hoped that he was headed for a career in research. He would be an excellent candidate."

"Is there anything else you remember about Josef?" asked George.

"Only the young man who was with him. I believe that they had just met at the seminar, but by the time it was completed, they were like best friends. I think that it was their mutual interest in the subject matter that drew them together, but I had the feeling they shared a number of other similarities as well."

"Do you remember the name of the other man?" asked George.

"I'm not sure about his last name," said Dr. Thorn, "but I believe his first name was Boris."

"Thank you very much for taking the time to speak with me," said George. "I'll pass on your kind words to Josef when I see him.

I'm sure he'll appreciate them. Thank you, also, for the handout. I'm sure it will be helpful. Good-bye."

George and his driver got back in the jeep for the return trip to the embassy. On the trip back, George carefully read the handout that he had been given. About halfway through the list, he knew that his trip had been worthwhile. The sixth disease listed resulted from the bite of a snake found only in a remote region of India. The balance of the discussion was all too familiar. This was the proof he needed that both men knew about the snake venom. It was beginning to look as if Josef had probably procured it He just needed to find out how, when, and why. He also needed to find out how much Josef knew about why Boris wanted the venom.

CHAPTER 35

From what George had learned about Josef since he arrived in Afghanistan, he was beginning to have serious questions in his mind. If Josef turned out to be the one who had procured the venom, was he even aware of what Boris had in mind to do with it? Nothing that he had heard about Josef made him sound even remotely like a person who would be involved in murder.

It was late when they got back to the embassy. Omar had anticipated that it might be and had prepared a room for George to spend the night there rather than drive back to his hotel. They would meet in the morning following breakfast to go over the information that George had obtained.

Before going to bed, George went over everything he had learned since he arrived in Afghanistan. Finding the fake bottom in the file drawer in Josef's work area with copies of the documents containing the missing cargo certainly indicated that Josef was at least Boris's accomplice in the theft of the cargo. It also seemed apparent that he was at least involved in obtaining the venom and getting it to Boris. His meeting with Dr. Thorn disclosed that Josef knew how to handle the venom and what it would do to anyone coming in contact with it.

The next morning, he and Omar went over all of the information he had obtained. "I don't know why," said George, "but I just don't believe that Josef had any idea that Boris intended to use the venom to commit murder. I wish I could talk with him without arousing his suspicion."

"There may be a way," said Omar. "What if you approach him as a reporter writing a story on the missing cargo? You don't know what the cargo is or to whom it was being sent. You've learned that someone in the states has been arrested for stealing it and sending it to Afghanistan and that Josef was the one designated to receive it. Maybe he'll tell you what he was supposed to do with it. We can make sure that he doesn't have access to a phone to check out your story."

"That might work," said George. "I'll go to the hospital this afternoon. Thank you for your suggestion. I'll let you know what I find out."

By the time he returned to his hotel, George had decided what he would say to Josef. Omar provided him with an identification card showing him to be a writer for the *Washington Post*. He'd also called his friend at the hospital so that George would be shown to Josef's room and would not be disturbed during his interview.

George had decided not to let on that he knew anything about the fake bottom drawer in Josef's workspace or what he had discovered there.

When he arrived at the hospital, he was taken directly to Josef's room. Josef was watching TV when the door opened and George walked in. He looked to be in his mid-to late twenties with sandy-colored hair and green eyes that had a tendency to turn grey when he was scared or nervous. He was a small built man but not skinny. His leg was in a cast and was suspended by a couple of cables attached to a pulley attached above the bed. As

Josef turned his head from the TV to his visitor, George started talking.

"Hello," said George. "My name is George Kilburn. I'm on assignment with the *Washington Post*. Would you mind talking with me for a few minutes?"

"Hello," said Josef. "Why do you want to talk to me?" he asked cautiously. He was not sure what to make of this person from an American newspaper. He began to get nervous and felt vulnerable with his leg dangling in the air.

"You're Josef Danforth, aren't you?" asked George.

"Yes I am, but why do you want to talk to me?"

"You have a friend in the State of Virginia named Boris Urich, don't you?"

"Yes I do. What's this about?"

George noted the look on Josef's face and guessed he wanted to be just about anywhere other than there.

"Have you heard anything about some cargo that was delivered to the Kingman Corporation warehouse by mistake?"

"Some people were talking about it in the hall the other day," said Josef. "What does that have to do with whether I know Boris?"

George noticed that a few drops of perspiration had formed on Josef's upper lip. "It's very simple," said George. "Boris was recently arrested for sending some cargo here rather than where it was supposed to go. Since the code on the shipping documents indicated that it was being sent to you, I wanted to get your side of the story. Will you talk with me?"

"This has to be a mistake," said Josef, clearly upset over the direction the conversation was taking. "Boris wouldn't steal anything. He's an honest man. He has a friend whose birthday is this week. He had a surprise for him and asked if I would mind receiving it so that it would get to the correct person."

"Only one set of shipping documents was found in Boris's possession," said George, "listing the shipment without the cargo in question. I've been told that the documents that arrived with the shipment and marked to your attention also didn't include the cargo in question. Can you explain that?"

"I told him his idea wouldn't work," said Josef, shaking his head and looking very upset. "I told him, but he wouldn't listen to me."

"Do you know what he was sending to his friend?" asked George.

"No, he didn't tell me," said Josef. "He just said that it was a gift for a friend. He listed it as 'cargo' just so that it wouldn't look suspicious to anyone else. It was just something that his friend had wanted and he had found locally. He's not a thief. He's a good person." Josef kept repeating.

"Why don't you tell me what happened from the beginning."

"I told him that he should just pay to send his friend's birthday present," said Josef. "He said that the government could well afford to let him make one shipment to a friend. He said that he had worked it all out so that neither of us would get caught. Boris sent me a set of shipping documents that included the cargo. When I got the package, I was supposed to just swap the documents he sent me with those that came with the delivery, but since I was here in the hospital when the delivery came, I couldn't do that.

"He said that when the cargo was put in the warehouse, he had arranged for it to be picked up by truck to be delivered to his friend. Apparently, a delivery driver had whatever he needed to make the delivery, but I don't know who that was."

"If I write this out, will you be willing to sign it?" asked George. "I can't promise anything, but I'll try to help you. I believe you're telling me the truth."

"Yes, I'll sign it. I guess that it wasn't a birthday present after all, was it?"

"It wasn't a birthday present," said George. "You said that you were sent a set of documents that included the cargo. Do you still have those documents?"

"Yes," said Josef. "They're in my file cabinet at work." Josef told George about the false bottom in his file cabinet.

"Have you known Boris for a long time?" asked George.

"I met him at a seminar we attended in San Francisco," Josef went on to tell George about the seminar. "Because of his background, the seminar held a special significance for Boris."

"What do you mean?"

"Boris had lost his mother to a disease that no one had identified until it was too late. It killed her. He was determined to learn everything he could about diseases that killed."

George remembered that Jordan and Sasha had found out Boris's mother had died of cancer and realized that apparently, Boris had altered the facts about his mother's death when he met Josef so Josef would think it only natural Boris was so passionate in his quest for learning all about diseases that killed.

"I thought Boris's mother didn't die until he was in medical school," said George.

"That's true," said Josef, "but she was sick for a long time before then, and they didn't know why."

Josef said that following the seminar, he had returned to India to study with Dr. Thorn until he was able to begin medical school at Med Start Junior College in Dover, Maryland. Boris was also attending Med Start, so they found themselves studying together again.

"Boris didn't finish Med Start," said Josef. "His grades dropped, but I think that was also around the time his mother died, so I'm not sure of his actual reason for leaving. I graduated from Med Start and then from Johns Hopkins."

"Since you graduated from medical school, why aren't you working as a doctor?" asked George.

"I wanted to return to India to set up a family practice in one of the primitive areas where they had no one to help them. I've always wondered if my family could have been saved if there had been a doctor in the area where they lived. However, I quickly learned that having a practice in a primitive area doesn't generate enough money to cover my student loans."

"So what did you do?"

While Josef was talking, George could tell from the tremor in Josef's voice and the way he was blinking back tears that he was truly upset over this and had honestly believed what Boris had told him.

"Boris was working in the shipping department at Higby International Freight Company in New Jersey, and he helped me get a job there. He's been a good friend to me, and I owe him a lot."

"Do you know if Boris is still interested in medicine?" asked George. He's obviously not a doctor or studying medicine now."

"I thought that he was going into medical research for a while," said Josef. "After Dr. Thorn's seminar, I thought he was doing some clinical research because he wrote and asked me to see if I could get a vial of some snake venom that we had studied about and send it to him. I was working and studying under Dr. Thorn at the time. Dr. Thorn had a number of vials of the venom that he used for his research, and I didn't think that he would mind if I sent Boris one since he had encouraged both of us to go into research. After I sent it, I never heard from Boris again about the snake venom.

"The next time I heard from him was when he got me the job in New Jersey. I made enough to pay most of my school loans. I moved back here to study and work with Dr. Thorn. My job with Kingman Corporation allows me to help my family and work from time to time with Dr. Thorn. Am I in a lot of trouble because of this?"

"I'm pretty sure that you are, but I'll try to minimize that. Your signed statement should help," said George.

After obtaining Josef's signed statement, George called Omar on his cell phone and let him know what had transpired and how helpful Josef had been. Omar promised that after all this was settled, he would speak with Dr. Thorn and see if something could be worked out to help Josef get into medical research and maybe obtain some outside work to help with his family situation.

That afternoon, George met with Stanley Fremont to let him know how everything had turned out. George told him that while Josef had had a part in what had happened, he felt Josef had been an unwilling accomplice in it.

Stanley told George that when it all came out in the press, and he was sure that it would, Josef would probably be able to get off with an official letter being placed in his file and possibly a fine. The fact that he had been so willing to admit his part and tell George where he had hidden the documents Boris had sent him would go a long way in his favor.

George made copies of the documents he had taken and left them with Stanley. They would be included in Josef's personnel file along with a copy of his signed statement. The originals were going back to Virginia to become a part of the file that was to be presented to the oversight committee and used in the criminal proceedings against Boris.

George doubted that they would ever find the truck driver who was supposed to pick up the cargo or learn who was supposed to receive it. It would need to be enough just to know the operation had been thwarted.

The only thing left to do now was to arrange for the cargo to be packed and put on the plane the next morning. Omar had arranged for that. Having the call come from the embassy assured that there would be no problems with his booking passage at the last minute.

When George returned to his room at the hotel, he stopped at the front desk to let them know he would be leaving the next morning and settle his bill. Back in his room, he called Trevor and Shaun on his cell phone and told them both everything that had happened. He said he and the cargo would be back the next day along with the evidence he had gathered. Shaun assured him that there would be a corporate van with an armed guard waiting to take charge of the cargo upon arrival. He told them they need not be concerned about his own transportation from the airport. He had that covered.

The next call was the one he was most anxious to make. Taking the time difference into account, he figured that Jordan would soon be taking her lunch break.

CHAPTER 36

The morning had gone by slowly for Jordan. She was almost finished with her report. She had not heard from George for several days, but knew that he had been very busy and had needed to stay focused on what he was doing. Both she and Trevor had completed their portions of this investigation unless and until George needed some additional documents or needed one of them to perform a task. She was just about to check with Sasha to see if she was interested in going to lunch when her phone rang.

"Hello? Jordan Anderson speaking."

"That's the best piece of news that I've heard all day," said a familiar voice. "I'm so glad to know that I haven't dialed the wrong number."

"George!"

He didn't have to be there to know that she had a huge smile on her face. He could feel it all the way in Afghanistan.

"How are you? I've missed hearing from you. Are you having any problems there? Is there anything you need me to send?"

"Hi yourself, beautiful. I've missed you too. Things are going just fine here, but there's one thing I'd like you to do."

"Name it." she said.

"Are you going to be busy tomorrow afternoon around four o'clock?" he asked.

"No, I'm free then. What do you need?"

"If you don't mind, I could use a ride home from the airport," he said.

"You're done there?" she asked.

"Yes. I've gotten everything that we need, including the missing cargo. I've spoken with Shaun. He'll have a corporate van waiting at the airport for the cargo. They offered me a ride, but I said that I thought I already had one. That is, if it isn't too much trouble."

"Are you kidding?" said Jordan. "I'll be there. I'm really glad you're coming home."

"I told Trevor to clear the following day for the three of us to gather everything for a presentation to the oversight committee," George said.

They talked on for a while longer just soaking in the sound of each other's voice until George finally said that if he was going to be ready to leave, he was hanging up to take care of some last-minute details.

When Jordan came out of her office to go to lunch with Sasha, she was almost floating. She was both happy and relieved. She couldn't have stopped smiling if her life had depended on it.

"I take it you heard from George," said Sasha with a laugh. "From the look on your face, it must have been good news."

"He's coming home tomorrow!" said Jordan. "He said he'd gotten everything he needed plus the missing cargo and he's coming home. Let's go get pizza. I'm starved."

When he boarded the plane the next morning, George noticed that there were already passengers in their seats. He had wondered if Kabul was the originating location for his flight. When he saw other passengers already seated, he realized it was not. When he had an opportunity later, he would ask one of the flight attendants where the flight had begun. It didn't matter, but it was just the kind of trivial information that George liked to know. He felt like it kept his mind busy and kept him from growing bored.

They had been flying for most of the day when George noticed what he thought was a change in the flight crew's demeanor. He couldn't be certain, but they seemed preoccupied and a little nervous. Earlier, they had served an excellent meal and, afterwards, gathered up all of the dishes and stowed everything away in the galley. Now, two of the attendants were going throughout the plane checking to make sure all compartments were latched shut and there were no loose items lying around. They were moving at a fast pace, and there were no smiles or inquiries as to whether a passenger would like a pillow for their head. The captain had turned on the "fasten seat belts" sign and had made a short announcement that they may be encountering some turbulence. However, the flight had remained very calm and smooth. George looked out the window. All he could see was water. They were traveling across the Atlantic, but he had no way of knowing where, over the Atlantic, they were.

A few minutes later, the captain's voice came over the loud speaker. "Ladies and gentlemen, you'll notice we've turned on the 'fasten seat belts' sign. I must ask you to remain in your seats. We have a slight situation that we believe will be remedied shortly. I'm sure it's nothing for you to be concerned about, so please bear with us. Thank you."

George wasn't sure what to think about this announcement. Apparently, George thought, neither did the other passengers. Some took the news in stride while others were visibly upset. One woman held her baby close to her heart and gently rocked back and forth in her seat while a tear made a path down her cheek.

It seemed like a long time, but it was in fact just a matter of a few minutes later when the captain's voice again came over the loud speaker. "Ladies and gentlemen, good news. The problem we were having was a lack of fuel. Apparently, at the last destination, the ground crew was supposed to have added fuel but for some unknown reason failed to do so. We're pretty sure that none of you brought along bathing suits for a swim in the Atlantic, so we've found an airport that can accommodate us. We'll be diverting to Gander, Newfoundland, to obtain more fuel. I assure you that we have plenty of fuel to reach that destination. So please relax and enjoy the rest of the flight. There will be no extra charge for this side trip. Since this will make us late for our arrival in Washington, we've radioed ahead to advise Dulles of our situation. If any of your travel plans call for changing planes to continue your journey, those planes will be notified and held until we arrive. Thank you for flying with us."

As the captain had planned with his announcement, the passengers chuckled about his humorous reference to swimming in the Atlantic. The balance of the trip went without incident. They refueled and were quickly back in the air, heading for home.

Jordan had arrived at the airport at the appointed time and noticed when she checked the schedule board that the plane was to be late arriving. She went to the reservation desk. "Excuse me," she said. I noticed that the plane from Afghanistan is showing a late arrival. Can you tell me if there's a problem and how late it will be?"

"I believe it's some kind of fuel problem," said the clerk. "I wouldn't worry, though. It's been worked out. It shouldn't be too late."

Jordan tried to keep her cool and to realize that this situation was causing the clerk a lot of extra stress with people coming to her for answers, but she couldn't help being concerned.

Finally, the announcement came over the loudspeaker that the flight from Afghanistan had landed and people could meet the arriving passengers after they passed through customs.

After what seemed like an eternity, Jordan saw George coming out of customs. Until she saw him, she didn't realize she had been holding her breath. All of the pent-up feelings she had been carrying ever since he had left came rushing at her. For a moment, she wasn't sure that her legs would hold her up. Fortunately, she was standing next to a heavy metal signpost indicating that this was where the security gates were located. She leaned against it and, placing one hand behind her, held on until she regained her equilibrium again. She took several deep breaths to bring her breathing back to normal so that George would not see how very worried she had been.

CHAPTER 37

George came out of customs, collected his baggage and turned the claim check for the cargo over to the Kingman Corporation representative. He had not let Jordan out of his sight since he arrived.

She knew that he had to take care of these tasks before he would be free to properly greet her.

As they walked away from the baggage claim area, George led her by her arm to an empty and somewhat secluded area out of the path of the throngs of people. He set his luggage down and turned toward Jordan.

In one swift motion, he pulled her into his arms and, holding her tightly with one arm, tilted her face up so that he gazed into her eyes. Never had he seen eyes that held so much love. He gently lowered his lips and placed a trail of kisses across her forehead and along the line of her jaw to her neck. Her hands were momentarily confined against his chest, but as he shifted slightly, they moved upward to circle his neck. She locked her fingers together as if she were afraid that he might let go of her. She had no intention of allowing him to let her go. His eyes locked with hers as he took command of her lips. As his tongue outlined her mouth, her lips parted in an invitation for him to delve deeper. A small whimper escaped from her throat. He felt her go up on her toes, pulling him even closer. He needed no further incentive. His kiss had begun gently but escalated rapidly as the fire that had been put on hold for so long flared to life. His tongue explored every bit of her mouth, thrusting in and out, merging with hers as they each probed the other with an urgency that could no longer be denied. Remembering that they were still standing in the airport baggage claim area, he gently pulled away from her, though it took every bit of strength that he could muster.

As he gazed into her loving eyes, he said, "I can't tell you how much I've missed you."

With a smile that was as bright as the sun, she replied, "You just did."

When they reached the parking lot, Jordan handed her car keys to George. He stowed his luggage in the trunk and opened the passenger door for Jordan. As she was about to enter, he kissed her again.

Since neither of them had eaten much that day, they decided to stop on the way home for dinner. George had a favorite restaurant in DC overlooking the Potomac River. He ordered the buffet for both of them, and they were shown to a table with a beautiful view overlooking the river.

During dinner, they limited their discussion to everyday events, having agreed to leave any talk of the investigation until they had had a chance to unwind and deal with the feelings and emotions they were experiencing. They had not fully realized the depths of the feelings they had for one another; all their discussions and time together thus far had been kept lighthearted and mainly limited to the investigation. That was about to change.

By the time they had finished their meal, George was having a difficult time staying awake. Jet lag was catching up with him.

Even though they didn't want to part, they agreed they needed to make it an early night.

George wasn't happy about Jordan driving herself home alone, but since they were in her car, there was no alternative.

They pulled up in front of his home, and he got his luggage out of the trunk. Jordan had walked around to the driver's side and was standing next to the open door. George handed her her keys, took her in his arms, and kissed her good night.

As Jordan drove away, George picked up his luggage and went inside. He was really looking forward to sleeping in his own bed again.

The next day, Jordan was in her office bright and early. The sun was shining. She realized she had slept better than she had in quite a while. She was pulling everything together for the meeting with George and Trevor when Sasha walked in.

"Good morning," she said. "Did George get back all right?"

"Yes he did. There was a slight hitch concerning his return trip, however."

Sasha looked at Jordan with a concerned expression. She didn't know if what was coming was good or bad.

"Don't worry," said Jordan when she noticed Sasha's concern. "George is fine. It's just that the plane almost ran out of fuel over the Atlantic. The pilot had to find someplace to make an emergency landing."

"You're kidding!" said Sasha. "They ran out of fuel?"

"They didn't actually run out, but they were running low," said Jordan, "and, apparently, didn't have enough to return all the way back here. I understand that things were a little tense until the pilot announced that he had found a place to land and refuel. Things at the airport were more than tense. This is one of those situations that, when they're happening, are scary but in the future, after everything has been worked out satisfactorily, makes a good 'remember when' story."

"Maybe so," said Sasha. "I just hope I never have an experience like that. I can do without a good 'remember when' story of that kind."

"We'll be meeting in the conference room at ten this morning," said Jordan. "I think I have everything we need set up, but maybe you could get a pitcher of ice water and some glasses to have on the table. After we break for lunch, I believe Shaun will be joining us."

"I'll get right on it," said Sasha.

Jordan put a hand on Sasha's shoulder. "I just want you to know that much of what we have and will accomplish with this case is because of you. If you hadn't cared enough to be concerned when you saw and heard things that you felt weren't right and hadn't had the courage to act on those feelings, this case might have had a very different ending. It certainly wouldn't have gone as smoothly as it has.

I'm very happy you confided in Boyd and that he had had enough faith in me to suggest that you call. You've caused some major changes in my life, and for that, I'm very grateful. I know I promised that I wouldn't let anyone know that you had contacted me before this investigation had officially begun, and I'll keep that promise if you want, but I wish you would reconsider and allow me to share this with Shaun, George, and Trevor. You deserve credit for all that you've done throughout this investigation, and that includes our initial contact. Please think about it. Will you?"

Sasha looked at Jordan, who could see tears in her eyes. "Thank you, Jordan. That's about the nicest thing anyone has ever said to me. Coming from you, it means a lot. I guess it would be all right if they knew now. Shaun should probably be told. After all, I did discuss company business with you that I wouldn't have known about if I hadn't been his private secretary. Please don't let it go any further, though."

"I promise you I won't," said Jordan, "and I'm sure you won't be in any trouble with Shaun over what you shared with me in the beginning."

Jordan gave Sasha a hug. "It's a quarter till ten. I'll finish up in the conference room, and you can get the ice water."

CHAPTER 38

A minute or so before ten o'clock, George and Trevor walked into the conference room laughing. George had just finished telling Trevor how close he had come to swimming in the Atlantic.

They took a couple of minutes to greet each other and to get coffee from the side table before moving to the conference table. On the wall next to the conference table was a whiteboard, with markers and an eraser, on which Jordan had outlined each of the charges followed by what they had obtained to prove the charge.

"Will Shaun be joining us?" Trevor asked, directing his question to Jordan.

"Not until after lunch," she replied. "He has two meetings this morning that he couldn't get out of. He'll be with us for the rest of the day, though."

"What we need to do this morning," began George, "is to lay out in detail each charge that we're pursuing connected to the theft and misdirection of the highly classified, security cargo that turned up at the Kingman warehouse in Afghanistan instead of the Kingman warehouse in Seattle. We must also set forth the proof that we've obtained concerning each charge.

Separate from those charges but having a direct bearing on the carrying out of those charges is the death of Chester Rafferty, the former disbursement officer at the Kingman Corporation, Arlington warehouse. We're alleging that Chester Rafferty didn't die of natural causes as was originally stated in the death certificate, but was murdered in order that Boris Urich would be placed in the position of disbursement officer with the intent of carrying out the above charges concerning the theft of cargo."

They began with the day that cargo had erroneously shown up at the Kingman warehouse in Afghanistan. Since the cargo had been a classified security system for U.S. ships along with the manuals and hardware to install it, if it had fallen into enemy hands, all U.S. ships and crews would have been at risk and billions of dollars could have been lost. The Senate oversight committee had gotten involved and immediately called for an investigation headed by its top investigator, George Kilburn. After word that the cargo, though unidentified, had turned up in Afghanistan was somehow leaked to the media, the decision was made to bring in a private investigator, Jordan Anderson, to assist in the investigation.

They methodically listed each step of their investigation, the evidence they had gathered, and the proof they had for each allegation.

A separate but intricate part of the investigation was the murder of Chester Rafferty, the disbursement officer at Kingman Corporation's Arlington warehouse. Chester was originally reported to have died from a massive heart attack. However, as the investigation progressed, it was found that he had been murdered by Boris Urich, the man who replaced him as the disbursement officer. The murder was almost not discovered until Jordan had found a medical examiner's report listing a rare, deadly, toxic substance that had been found in Chester's bloodstream. The substance could only be found in a snake that lived in a remote region of India. Further investigation by Jordan disclosed that the autopsy had revealed a puncture mark on Chester's neck that was determined to be the entry way for the poison.

They listed the information they had on the individuals who were under suspicion, including personal internet searches and where or to whom each search had led them. They included their trips to check out the schools attended and fields of study indicated by these people. They also located and visited the previous employers of the suspects. They found that when Boris came to work at Kingman, he failed to list his previous employment at Higby International Freight Company. This was because he had resigned from there to keep the fact that he had been accused of falsifying shipping documents to cover the theft of cargo from being made a part of his employment history. It was later revealed that he used the same tactics that he used at Higby to steal the classified security system that was the subject of this investigation.

George's trip to Afghanistan provided the last remaining piece to the puzzle, so to speak. Finding the missing documents in Josef's cabinet under a false bottom drawer and Josef's voluntarily signed statement setting forth his own part in the process and documenting his discussions with Boris provided all that was needed to bring criminal charges against Boris.

The team made doubly sure they had not omitted anything. When they broke for lunch, they decided on the local pizza restaurant which was in walking distance. During lunch, they shared humorous events and insights they had experienced along the way.

Jordan couldn't help noting how wonderful it felt to be with George and Trevor in a relaxed setting and how much she would miss it in the future once the case was completed. She hoped that they would want to remain in touch as friends, and she hoped for so much more with George.

Shaun joined them in the conference room after lunch. They brought him up to speed with all they had covered. He knew that they had accomplished a lot, as he had been kept informed piece by piece during the investigation. However, having everything laid out in preparation for going before the Senate oversight committee was impressive.

"I believe," said George in summation, "that this will be more than enough to convict Boris Urich of espionage, treachery, and theft of government property.

The second charge of murder doesn't come under the jurisdiction of the Senate oversight committee," said George. "I would suggest contacting the FBI," he said, addressing his comment to Shaun. "There's no question this is a federal case since the venom came from out of the country. If they aren't the ones to handle the case, they'll know who to direct you to. I suspect that the State Department may also want to get involved in this. I'm sure that we have everything needed to prove the case, and we'll be happy to hand over the evidence to them.

"They'll be looking for means, motive, and opportunity, and we have proof of all three. Boris had the means when he asked for and received the venom from Josef. There is also proof of his medical training and specifically of the venom being sent to him by Josef. His motive was clear; Rafferty had had him fired from his previous job, and assuming Rafferty's job put him in the position to carry out the theft. I have no doubt that whoever prosecutes this case will be able to tie down when and how Boris actually carried out the murder, especially if his admission will get him life rather than the death penalty."

"I'll contact the FBI today," said Shaun. "We owe each of you a huge amount of gratitude. I've never seen a team that works as well as the three of you."

"I'd like to add something," said Jordan. "There's one more person who must share in your praise, Shaun. That's Sasha. Not only has she gone way beyond the call of just doing her job with everything we asked of her, she also took the initiative and made suggestions that have proven to be extremely helpful. Also, I must share one final thing that none of you is aware of."

All eyes turned to her.

"Sasha had come to me on her own before any of you were in the picture and before the story was leaked to the press. She said she had seen and heard little things that had made her afraid there was something very wrong going on, but she didn't know what it was. She was afraid to go to you, Shaun, simply because she had nothing but her gut feelings to go on and she couldn't bring herself to look foolish in your eyes. She holds you in very high esteem, and she made it clear from the start she knew you wouldn't be involved in anything that wasn't on the up and up.

"She was willing to pay me herself as a PI to look into this matter. She assured me that if I found nothing was wrong, that it was just her imagination, she'd tell you what she had done regardless of the consequences. That took a lot of bravery on her part."

All three men were speechless. Finally, Shaun broke the silence by saying he had never had or known an employee who showed such loyalty as Sasha had. He would make sure that Sasha received a commendation and a large bonus. He said he knew she didn't want any public display and would keep his action between the two of them. He turned to Jordan. "I for one don't care how you got involved in this case. I just thank God you did." He returned to his office to phone the FBI.

George started to say something, but nothing would come out. He just sat there shaking his head in disbelief.

Trevor looked from George to Jordan and, finally, just started laughing. He gave George a slap on the shoulder. "I guess I'll head back to the office and arrange a time for the presentation before the Senate oversight committee," he said as he got up to leave the room. "I imagine that I'll be seeing you around, Jordan," he added.

There were only the two of them left in the room. Jordan said, "Please say something. I know I probably should have told you sooner, but I promised Sasha I wouldn't involve her without her permission. There was no way to tell you without involving Sasha. It was only this morning that she agreed to allow me to say something. I couldn't allow her to not receive any credit when she'd done so much. Please don't be mad at me."

"Mad at you? How could you think I'm mad at you? You're the best investigator I've ever worked with, not to mention the most beautiful and loving. You paid me a high compliment with what you said. Anyway, I don't know how to be mad at someone when I'm totally in love with her."

"Do you really mean that?" asked Jordan. "I hope so, because I'm totally in love with you too!"

George reached out his hand to Jordan. "Let's get out of here so I can show you just how much I love you. I sincerely hope you don't have any plans for the next fifty or sixty years. If you do, you're going to have to cancel them because I plan to keep you very occupied."

"As much as I like the sound of that," said Jordan, "I hope that you don't plan to ask me to stop being an investigator. That's something I love too."

"You don't have anything to worry about there. From what Trevor has told me, several offices on the Hill are already competing to convince you to work with them. You just won't be able to work for Senator Granger, that is, unless you get me fired first. There's a rule against married couples working for the same boss."

Due to the way George was looking at her, Jordan felt the heat in the room rise by about thirty degrees. She had never seen so much love, and it was almost more than she could imagine that it was being directed at her. She knew without a doubt that her life had just taken a turn in a beautiful direction.

"But George," said Jordan with a smile, "I'm not married."

"Not yet!" he replied with a gleam in his eye. "Not yet!"

EPILOGUE

A few months later, George and Jordan were sitting on the couch in the living room of their new home. They were reading an article in the newspaper about the case George had presented to the oversight committee. Its main concerns were addressed when the members were assured that the people involved in the theft had been apprehended and turned over to the FBI for prosecution and that the Naval Advanced Early Warning Security System had been fully retrieved without being copied or compromised.

Shaun had contacted the FBI and turned over every piece of evidence that the team had acquired concerning the theft of the navy cargo and the murder of Chester Rafferty. The FBI had absolutely no trouble turning the information and documents they received into an airtight case of espionage and murder against Boris Urich. They thought that he would probably receive life in prison with no chance of parole, if not the death sentence.

As Trevor had predicted, several offices on the Hill offered Jordan jobs. She had not made a decision on those offers because she had an issue that was a much higher priority. She and George had gotten married and were expecting their first child.

The last remaining hurdle had dissolved faster than butter on hot popcorn. Annie had accepted and bonded with George. Jordan found out that he had used bribery to get close to Annie in a hurry by making sure that he always carried a few of her favorite treats in his pocket.

Printed in the United States
By Bookmasters